EYES WIDE OPEN

A NOVELLA

Eyes Wide Open

A Novella

Jan Miklaszewicz

Copyright © 2025 by Jan Miklaszewicz

All rights reserved.

No part of this book may be reproduced, distributed, or transmitted in any form or by any means, including photocopying, recording, or other electronic or mechanical methods, without the prior written permission of the author, except as permitted by US copyright law.

No generative artificial intelligence (AI) was used in the creation of this book. The author expressly prohibits the use of this publication as training data for AI technologies or large language models (LLMs) for generative purposes. The author reserves all rights to license uses of this work for generative AI training and the development of LLMs.

All of the names, characters, and incidents portrayed herein are fictitious. No identification with actual persons (living or deceased), places, buildings, or products is intended or should be inferred.

Cover and interior by Jan Miklaszewicz

ISBN: 9798280162150

Author's Note

Given the genre, perhaps it should go without saying that this story has some grisly scenes. However, specific trigger warnings can be found on the Eyes Wide Open page of my website: janmiklas.blogspot.com

Prologue

If this were a horror movie, he'd be shouting at the screen right now, and one of the lads, most likely James, would be launching into a speech about how these things wouldn't work without bad decision-making. But it's not a horror movie, and it's not a dream either, as far as he can tell. No, it's just him at the top of the cellar stairs in the wee small hours, terrified out of his wits.

And going down into the musty darkness seems the most natural thing in the world, and how crazy is that? There are plenty of better options. He could go back to bed. He could make himself a snack. He could turn the TV up so loud that Sharon or Claire will come down and give him an earful. But no. For whatever reason, he's going into the cellar, one creaking stair at a time, the damp air wrapping around his naked legs like he's climbing into a pool of icy water.

At the bottom, some unnameable horror awaits. He

knows it in the same way you know it's not safe to fart. And it won't be some loony with a machete or some murderous clown. No, it'll be a thing. Some vile creature from a place of nightmares. And there'll be no violin strings to ratchet up the tension, no camera to cut away from the final, graphic act. This is all going to happen in real time, and he's walking down to meet it, eyes wide open.

His left foot hits the age-warped linoleum of the cellar floor, and mingling with the smell of mildew is something wretched and unclean. Excrement and rotting meat, and the fluid that seeps from leg ulcers, that sickening sweetness he once encountered when visiting his great-aunt in an old people's home. And with it comes the rasping sound of approaching death, the awful maraca shake of a rattlesnake's tail, and somehow both of these things seem to be coming from inside him.

And now he realises that he's weeping, silent tears running down his face and dripping from the point of his chin. What on earth is he doing in this godforsaken place? And yes, there it is, he's literally filling his boxer shorts now, his crotch and inner thighs hot and stinging as his bowel and bladder betray him. Then an icy hand closes around his heart, and he screams so hard that something rips inside his throat.

One

Hartmouth is a lovely little place, warm in the summer and fairly mild in the winter. It has a decent seafront with a newly refurbished lido, a passable town centre with several good cafes and bars, and a university in the middle third of the latest league table. And despite complaints from locals that it's been ruined by an influx of students, the quality of life here remains far above the national average.

Luke certainly likes it well enough, and so do the rest of his housemates, even Stanley up there in the so-called penthouse with its crappy little terrace. Then again he's one of those mature students, plus he doesn't drink, so his opinion doesn't count for much either way.

"Hey, Sharon," he calls from his spot on the living room's main three-seater sofa, a shapeless corduroy thing that's seen more action than all of the residents put together. "Grab me another beer, will you?"

"Me too," adds James from the mismatched armchair. "In fact, might as well bring the whole box."

In the kitchen, Sharon rolls heavily made-up eyes at Sadie, who's standing just outside the back door enjoying the last of the spliff she saved from last night's session. "They'll be pissed out of their brains by tea time."

"Nothing new there," says Sadie, brushing stray flecks of ash from her jeans and zipped hoodie. "If you can't beat them, though… Any of that wine left?"

"Third of a bottle, and there's this lemon stuff as well." Sharon reaches into a fridge devoid of anything but booze and a few sad salad items. "Here, take these through and I'll bring the rest."

Sadie flicks the dead spliff into the yard and grabs the box of strong Belgian lager, then heads down the hallway, the floorboards squealing beneath the wafer-thin carpet. This place is a joke really, as are most of the other student houses she's seen. Landlords buy a fixer-upper, get a dodgy builder in, and four or five bedrooms suddenly become seven or eight. Quick lick of bargain basement paint, and Bob's your uncle, another money-spinner.

"You took your time," says Luke as she enters the living room. "Been lezzing it up again?"

"You've just got a thing for blondes."

"One track mind," says James. "Are you partaking?"

"Be rude not to, I suppose."

"You're not blonde anyway," says Luke. "Sharon is, but you're more or less ginger."

"And proud of it, you big old lump."

Sharon comes in and joins Sadie on the second sofa, which like the rest of the furniture looks sorely out of place. With their high ceilings and large bay windows, these grand old houses seem to cry out for something more upmarket.

"When's Charlie due back?" Luke asks. "I thought he'd be here by now."

"His dad's car got stolen," says Sharon, sloshing cheap Chardonnay into a pair of wine glasses. "So he's coming down on the train. And before you ask, I still haven't heard from Claire or Nao. I tried their mobiles, but they both went through to voicemail."

"Lezzing it up," says Luke through a mouthful of beer.

"Oh, for fuck's sake." Sadie shakes her head. "Just because a girl isn't throwing herself at you, doesn't mean she's a lesbian. Try being more like James. At least he keeps himself in shape and takes a shower once in a while."

"Uh, thanks, I think."

"Old curtains here is massively gay," says Luke, winking at his partner in crime. "That's the only reason girls talk to him. He's not a threat like me."

"You're hardly a threat," says Sadie. "More like a weapon."

***

Charlie, often teased by his housemates for his plummy accent and regal bearing, steps off the train at Hartmouth station at quarter to four. It's been a pleasant little break, Christmas and New Year with the family, but he's glad to be back for the next semester. And when he spots Claire and Naoka at the taxi rank, he very nearly jumps for joy.

"Room for one more?" he asks, his entire face a smile.

"Depends who's paying, your highness." Claire embraces him in a motherly hug, her perfume making his eyes water. "Were you on the Express?"

"Yes, of course. Hello, Nao."

"Hey, Charlie," she says, her Scots brogue as strange as ever, coming from the mouth of a girl who looks fully Japanese. "Have you put on weight?"

"I don't think so."

"We had an empty seat at our table the whole time," says Claire. "You could've come and joined us."

"Well, I would if I'd known."

The taxi driver hurries them along, and soon their bags are onboard and they're off to Cromwell Lane, over on the west side of town. As they reach Lyme Street, Claire asks the driver to stop at the Bestmart so they can pick up a few supplies, and she and Naoka come back five minutes later laden with booze and snacks.

"Sorry about that, driver."

"No skin off my nose." He pulls the taxi into what little traffic there is on a wintry Sunday afternoon. "Meter's running anyway."

"What are the chances," says Charlie, "that the others are as drunk as lords already?"

"Pretty high, I'd say."

"We'll find out soon enough," says Claire. "My money's on Luke being the worst, then Sades, James, and Sharon."

"What about Stanley?"

"Oh, come on, Charlie. The last time he had a drink was... well, has he ever had a drink?"

"James thinks he does it in secret," he says. "Got himself a little stash of the good stuff up in his room."

"And a stack of dirty magazines."

"Oh, he's alright," says Naoka. "Just a wee bit stiff, that's all."

"Here we are then, folks. Cromwell Lane."

"Just past the big Sycamore there." Claire leans forward and points at the house. "The one with the spiked iron railings."

Charlie hands the driver a twenty, the two girls vowing to square him up later once they've worked out his share of the Bestmart haul. Then they clamber out onto the street, their bags in tow, and look with affection at their home for the next six months. An imposing Victorian terraced affair and rather the worse for wear, but the site of a hundred fabulous memories and surely several hundred more to come.

Two

Less than two weeks into the new semester, Stanley has already been given his first assignment. An ethnographic study based on the work of a North American sociologist. It's a bit light on theory, which is a shame, but the chance to observe people in a social setting is nonetheless enlightening. The way their speech and body language betray their attitudes and desires, etcetera, etcetera.

Initially he wanted to study his housemates. Claire's attempts to make light of being so overweight. Conventionally beautiful Sharon playing it cool around conventionally handsome James. Sadie's hard-bitten exterior masking the pain of family tragedy. But it would only lead to hurt feelings if they got wind of it, so instead he's chosen the cafe up on Lyme Street.

And here he sits on a wet Thursday afternoon, chain smoking hand-rolled cigarettes and drinking thin black coffee, notebook at the ready. From what he can gather, there's some kind of mental health centre nearby, going by the weirdness of half the clientele. They come in and order their sandwiches and baked potatoes, then chatter inanely at the owner until their medication kicks in and they start to zone out. Still, it gives him plenty of fodder for this assignment. The casual familiarity of the regulars versus the measured, polite deportment of the newcomers.

"Dreary weather, sir," the owner says as he clears the adjacent table. "Care for a top up?"

"I'm okay, thanks."

"Let's hope it's better for the eclipse, eh? Just our luck we won't be able to see a thing."

"..."

"First of the new millennium, they say. A group of us are heading down to the seafront on Sunday night. You're more than welcome to tag along."

"Uh, possibly, yeah."

"Sure you don't fancy a top up? I can do you a nice cheese toastie if you like."

"I'd better be off, actually. Maybe next time."

"Suit yourself, sir. Always happy to have your custom."

Stanley pays and leaves, discomfited by the owner's 1950s shopkeeper act. It may wash with the regulars, but once this assignment's done, he won't be going back again. There's quite enough nutty at number thirteen, thank you very much.

Crossing at the lights by the graveyard, daylight fading fast, he adjusts the strap of his shoulder bag, which has slipped from his narrow shoulder once too often, then turns down into Cromwell Lane. The bins are out for Friday morning's collection, and no doubt it will be him who ends up lugging theirs outside. Once he's sorted the recycling from the general waste, that is.

"Thank God you're back," says Sadie as he comes through the front door and into the gloom of the hallway. "The electricity's gone again."

"That Stan the man?" Luke calls from the kitchen. "Beer's starting to get warm."

"For God's sake," says Stanley. "Has Sharon been using those straighteners again?"

"Guilty," a voice calls from up on the first floor. "Sorry."

"Where's the torch, Sadie?"

"Batteries are dead. Luke was messing around with it the other night."

It's a wonder these twats can even tie their own shoelaces, he thinks as he reaches the cellar door at the end of the hallway, to the right of the kitchen. It's also a wonder this whole place doesn't go up in flames, judging by the state of the electrical panel. And what kind of moron would put the thing in the darkest, nastiest recess of the house?

"Here, hold this." He passes Sadie his bag then takes a cigarette lighter from his pocket. "I wish you lot would work out how to do this yourselves."

"If Stan the man can't," says Luke, appearing in the kitchen doorway and blocking what remaining daylight there is, "then no one can."

Stanley bites his tongue and opens the cellar door, a chill

waft of mouldy air coming up to greet him. Horrible place, really, and of no use to man or beast. The landlord should get the panel relocated then stick a bloody padlock on the door. Thankfully it's not all the way down at the bottom.

"Shout up to Sharon, will you?" he tells Sadie. "See if she's unplugged those straighteners."

She nips off and does as he asks, then returns with confirmation, quite unnecessarily, since he heard Sharon's dulcet tones with his own two ears.

"Okay, here goes." Stanley creaks down the first half dozen stairs and holds the lighter up to the panel on his left. The smell of mildew is stronger now and threatens to turn his stomach. He inspects the individual trips and resets the offending item before pushing the main circuit breaker back into position.

"Hallelujah," Luke shouts as the lights come on. "The beer has been saved."

"Thanks, Stanley," says Sadie.

"Come and take a look for yourself. It's not exactly rocket science."

"Way too dark."

"Turn the light on then. Just inside the door there."

Sadie flips the switch, an old bakelite thing, and right on cue the cellar lightbulb flares, then crackles and fizzles out. "Fuck that for a game of soldiers," she says.

Three

Sunday dawns fresh and bright, which is more than can be said for most of the housemates, who wake around noon with an assortment of hangovers, ranging from 'maybe I should take it easy for a while' to 'help, my eyes are bleeding'. But as the day wears on, they begin to emerge from their cocoons of post-binge misery, and by late afternoon the first few drinks have been poured. Half of them don't have classes on Monday morning anyway, so why the hell not?

"What time does Bestmart close?" Luke asks.

"Same as every Sunday since we've been here. Eight o'clock."

"Why thank you, James my boy. Because there's no way these beers are lasting me the night."

"I'm surprised you can afford to be drinking like that," says Naoka, sandwiched between Claire and Sharon on the second sofa. "Must have blown half your student loan by now."

"My finances are of no concern to you, my dear."

"Or to yourself, it seems."

"Well, yes, Nao. But continue to party I shall. You up for a beer run, James?"

"Maybe later."

"How about your good self, young majesty?" Luke digs an elbow into Charlie. "Care to sally forth on a quest for more beverages? I can't promise there'll be any dragons for you to slay."

"Alright then."

"I'll come too," says Claire. "If you can wait half an hour. Growing girl needs a bite to eat first."

"In fact, why don't we pile up the pub for a few?" Luke's face is a mask of enthusiasm. "I don't mind getting a couple of rounds in."

"The Slaughtered Lamb?"

"Come on, Sharon, it's not that bad. Maybe there's a happy hour."

"Misery hour, more like."

"Well, it can't be much worse than here, can it?"

"I guess we could," says Sadie. "Wouldn't mind a change of scenery, to be fair. Anyone want to go and invite him upstairs?"

"Invite me where?" asks Stanley, appearing in the doorway, his fine brown hair quite tidy for a change.

"Up the pub. But it looks like you're already heading out."

After telling them of his plan to watch the eclipse with a

classmate, he leaves them to it, though not before sharing a look with Naoka that causes Claire to raise an eyebrow. But it couldn't be, could it? She's barely seen them say two words to one another.

***

Just after seven o'clock, the door to number thirteen comes open and the tipsy occupants spill out onto the path, minus Sharon and Naoka. Pair of stick-in-the-muds would rather stay home and have an early night. Or a massive lezzing session, if Luke is to be believed.

"Bet we're the only ones in there, save for a few old farts," says James.

"Wouldn't surprise me," says Claire, already a little breathless as they make their way up the street. "But as long as there's vodka, I don't really care that much."

"That's the spirit, pardon the pun."

"Fucking hell, Charlie. You should buy the first round as punishment for that one."

"Sorry, Luke. Didn't mean to steal your crown."

"Cheeky little shit," he says, putting him in a playful headlock. "King takes prince. Checkmate."

"There aren't any princes in chess."

"Oh, sorry, Mr Kasparov."

And so they continue towards the pub, whose name not one of them can recall until they near the end of Lyme Street and take a left. The Red Lion. Hardly original, but there you have it, and there's nothing too original about the inside, either. Ten, maybe fifteen patrons, gaudy red carpet and dark wooden tables, and a wall-mounted jukebox over by a tired-looking pool table.

"What are you having then?" Luke asks the group. "Me and Charlie will get them in while you find us a place to sit."

"Vodka for me," says Claire. "Double with ice, and a bottle of Juicer. Mango if they've got it, but orange will do."

"White wine," says Sadie. "How about you, James? Pint of lager?"

"How did you guess? Luke, Charlie, we having a game of pool?"

"Might as well."

"What can I get for you, gentlemen?" asks the barman, who has just finished serving the middle-aged couple to their left. "And if you don't mind, I'm going to have to ask this young man for some form of identification."

"Can't you see he's royalty?" Luke asks.

"He does look quite princely, I'll give you that, but I still need to see some proof of age."

So Charlie presents his provisional driving license, and several minutes later they find the other three around the corner, at the far end of the pool table. James has already set the balls up and no doubt chosen the best cue for himself.

"Here you go, ladies," says Charlie, placing the metal drinks tray on the table.

"Such a sweetheart," says Claire.

"Guess who got asked for ID again," says Luke, taking his and James's pints from the tray and drinking deeply from his own.

"That's a tough one." Sadie pretends to think it over. "If it was mental age, it would've been you for sure. But I'm going to have to go with our little prince here."

***

The pub was far more fun than expected, and as they weave and croon their way back along Lyme Street, Luke comes up with the bright idea of taking a detour through the graveyard. That'll be a real story for the grandkids, eh? Creeping around all those statues and tombs during a lunar eclipse.

"Fuck it," says Charlie. "Let's do it."

"That's no language for royalty." Claire cackles and almost stumbles into the road. "What would your mother say?"

"Off with his naughty little head," says James. "Hey, look, they haven't even locked the gates. Come on."

"Last one in's a rotten egg."

"Fucking hell, Luke. Who even says that?"

"I says that, Sades. Come on. Let's see who can find the oldest gravestone."

And with that, the five of them shamble through the arched iron gates and make for the little chapel at the centre. A stiff breeze has blown up around them, and if they were to look up, they'd notice the alabaster moon already partly obscured, as though a bite has been taken out of it.

"Remember," says Luke. "First one to find a rotten gravestone is... wait, no, that's not right."

"Oldest gravestone."

"Thank you, my boy. That's the one. Well, none of these are very old, are they? Look, nineteen eighty-five, nineteen ninety-three."

"When's this thing supposed to be happening, by the way?" Charlie asks, finally looking at the sky. "Oh, it's already started."

Feeling the first few shivers of cold now, Sadie zips her hoodie and thrusts her hands into the pockets. "I'm pretty sure Stanley said eleven thirty for it to be completely covered."

"He did," says James. "Which is about twenty-five minutes from now."

After a smoke and pee break by the chapel, which includes Sadie getting her bare ass stung by nettles, they aim for the oldest-looking part of the graveyard. Not all that easy to tell, admittedly, what with the moonlight beginning to weaken, but as they push further, the gravestones do indeed become older, creeping back now towards the eighteenth century.

"I'm starting to think," says Claire, several paces behind and looking somewhat bedraggled, "that this was a terrible idea."

"Starting?" James laughs. "The only way it could be any more terrible is if one of us brought a ouija board."

"Don't fucking tell me you did," says Sadie, not a shred of humour in her voice. Dicking around in here is one thing, but actively trying to summon some kind of spirit is beyond the pale.

"I may be stupid, but I'm not that fucking stupid."

"Oh, look," says Charlie. "Seventeen sixty. Eloise Hubbard."

"You've got better eyesight than me."

"Hey, guys," Luke calls, having forged ahead to the graveyard's farthermost corner. "Come and check this one out."

Catching up with him in the ever-dwindling light, which now has a reddish tinge to it, they peer at a crooked old gravestone five or so metres away, almost buried amidst a twist of weeds and brambles.

"Sixteen something, this one," says Luke. "There doesn't seem to be a name."

"Yeah, just a date by the looks of it."

"Laugh my ass off if it was sixty nine."

"Why not go and check?" says Sadie. "It's the closest you'll ever get to one in real life."

"Alright then, but it's getting pretty dark. Got a lighter?"

"Hang on." She sparks up a cigarette and offers the pack around—no takers—before handing it to Luke.

"This is getting stupid," says Claire, several paces back in the dim red light. "Let's just go home."

"No point," Sadie replies. "It's going to be pitch black any minute now, so we'll have to stay put for a while."

"Go on then, mate," says James, who has now joined Claire and seems to have lost his sense of adventure. "Might as well check it out now you've dragged us all the way here."

Pissed as a fart or not, Luke senses the challenge in his housemate's words. No way did he drag them here, they came of their own accord, but whatever. So he picks his way through the brambles in the near blackness, trying his drunken best not to get torn to shreds.

"Be careful," says Charlie.

"No fucking shit." Luke strikes the lighter and pushes ever closer to the gravestone, beginning to realise just how foolish this whole thing is. "Okay, it's sixteen... it's sixteen... oh, shit." His laughter seems small and forced. "Sixteen sixty-nine. What did I tell you?"

Then a breath of wind snuffs the lighter out, and the next moment he stumbles forwards, almost as if pulled off balance, the bridge of his nose colliding hard with the top of the gravestone. A raw flash of pain explodes in his head, and the red-hued gloom turns pure black as the moon is finally gobbled up.

Four

"Morning."

"Alright, Stanley?" Naoka glances up from the breakfast table, a six-chair pine number that's seen better days. "You're up early."

"I could say the same for you. It's usually as quiet as the grave down here at this time."

"Had a bad dream and couldn't get back to sleep."

"Nothing too sinister I hope," he says, taking a loaf of bread from the cupboard. "By the way, I couldn't help but notice..."

"The blood in the hallway?"

"Yeah."

"Long story."

Stanley puts a single slice of bread into a toaster so decrepit it ought to be condemned. "Go on."

"Luke had an accident. They were mucking about in the graveyard, and somehow he managed to break his nose."

"Deary me."

"Aye, it's not looking good. Insisted he didn't want to go to the hospital, though."

"He probably should. They might need to reset it."

"I expect he'll change his mind when he's sobered up. But aye, he came back bleeding like a stuck pig and continued to bleed all over the hallway and living room. Surprised you didn't hear it, the noise they were making."

"Didn't get back until two."

"Well, aren't we the dirty stop out?"

"Just a classmate."

"Hey, hen, didn't think we'd be seeing you for hours."

Claire comes into the kitchen, face puffy, eyes like pissholes in the snow. "Morning, Stanley."

"Morning," he says, gingerly prying his toast from the toaster and buttering it. "Sounds like you lot had quite a night."

"Ugh, it was ridiculous. Freezing our asses off in the pitch dark while Luke lost half a gallon of blood. Lucky for us, Sharon and Nao were still up when we got back."

"Maybe we should make it a rule," says Naoka. "At least one of us in the house has got to stay sober when the others are on a bender. Just in case something goes wrong."

"Don't look at me," says Stanley between mouthfuls of toast. "Never been much of a babysitter."

When he leaves, Claire makes coffee and joins Naoka at the table. "Thank God I've only got one lecture this afternoon. How drunk were we?"

"You weren't so bad, to be honest. A bit on the loud side,

but I think the shock of what happened sobered you up some."

"Weird, isn't it?" says Claire, rubbing gently at her temples. "You can be pissed out of your mind but seem quite normal to other people."

"Aye, right enough… Although there's nothing normal about running around a graveyard in the middle of the night. What on earth were you silly buggers thinking?"

***

The accident and emergency department at Hartmouth's Lady Rutherford Hospital is fairly quiet, the weekend rush now over. Through luck rather than judgement, Luke saved himself a wait of four or five hours by refusing to come in last night. Not that he'd recognise any sort of good news right now, waiting glumly for his X-ray results with the mother of all hangovers and a hideously painful face. His eyes are almost swollen shut, and he can barely breathe through either of his nostrils.

"Hello, my lovely," says the nurse. "Would you mind coming with me?"

He follows her to a consulting room and is offered a seat by one of the duty doctors, who explains that despite some nasty bruising and a minor laceration, there appears to be no lasting damage. No break, no surgery required, just regular fluids and painkillers to help keep the swelling at bay.

"Now," says the doctor, briefly consulting some paperwork. "It says on your questionnaire here that you'd been drinking at the time of the accident."

"Yeah," says Luke, trying to raise an eyebrow and instantly regretting it. "Stupid, I know."

"Any other injuries?"

"Only some scratches on my hands."

"Alright then. Well, you've taken quite a blow, and you're going to be in some discomfort for a while yet. If you experience any other problems—any dizziness or disturbance of your vision, beyond the obvious, of course—you should come and see us."

"Okay, doctor. Thank you."

"Take this to the dispensary," he says, tearing a scribbled prescription from his pad and handing it to Luke. "One of the receptionists will point you in the right direction."

And that is pretty much that. Twenty minutes later, Luke is in a taxi and heading back to Cromwell Lane. As they approach the graveyard on Lyme Street, he lowers his aching, blurry eyes and doesn't look up again until the taxi comes to a halt. He pays the driver and heads up the path, his heart as heavy as lead as he opens the door and steps inside.

Five

The rest of the week brings freezing temperatures and heavy snow, almost unheard of in these parts, plus a bout of diarrhoea and vomiting attributed to a Thai green curry cooked by Claire and Sadie.

"Hey, Sharon," says James, poking his head into the rarely used office, which sits between the living room and the kitchen. "You okay there?"

"Just trying to get a bit of work done."

"What's wrong with your room?"

"Radiator's on the blink," she says. "And there's not so many distractions in here."

"Oh, is that a hint?"

"Of course not. In fact, it feels like we've barely spoken recently."

James comes into the office, comprising a pair of desks along the far wall and another pair pushed together to make a central working space, where Sharon is sitting with her laptop and a pile of textbooks. With its sagging shelves and unadorned walls, the place bears all the hallmarks of a hurried afterthought.

"How's your stomach, anyway?" she asks as he sits across from her. "Still, you know…"

"No, not anymore, thank God. But Luke and Charlie have got it pretty bad."

"Oh dear."

"…"

"How is he, anyway?"

"Charlie?"

"No, Luke. I know I'm not his biggest fan, but the house feels dead without him holding court in the living room."

"I think he's feeling a bit down. First his nose, and it must hurt like hell—I mean, the whites of his eyes are almost solid red—then getting a bad stomach as well. But yeah, it does feel kind of dead here at the moment."

"Maybe we should try and get him out of his room. Get everyone together for a movie night or something."

"Yeah, that could—"

A sudden series of ceiling-shaking thuds rains dust upon them.

"What the hell?" says Sharon.

"Who the fuck is jumping around like that?"

The thudding has stopped now, but as they venture out to the bottom of the staircase, it starts again. They hurry upstairs and find a sleepy-looking Charlie outside the bathroom door.

"What's going on?" James asks.

"I don't know. Sounded like someone was having a fit in there."

Sharon joins Charlie, then knocks and calls out, at the same time trying the handle and finding it unlocked. She inches the door open just enough to peer inside and is surprised to find the room completely empty.

***

Naoka's second-floor window overlooks the narrow alley and the backs of the houses on Cranmer Lane, the next street over. It's not usually the most handsome of vistas—the crap that people keep in their yards is a constant source of amazement—but covered in snow like this, she might even call it picturesque. Probably the only benefit of the current weather, but at least it's something.

Turning her attention back to her laptop screen, death metal pounding from her earphones, she types out a speculative sentence then immediately deletes it. Basically saying the same as the previous one, just phrased in a slightly different way. Idle tautology, as Stanley likes to call it.

As the current track ends, she realises someone's knocking on her door. "Aye, come in," she calls, hitting pause and taking out her earphones. "It's not locked."

"Hey, just seeing if you're okay." Sharon steps into the room. "Didn't you hear the banging?"

"Banging? No. Unless it was me tapping my feet to Bucket of Satan Spunk."

"This was pretty full on."

Naoka shrugs. "Have you checked with the others?"

"Stanley and Sades are out," says James, appearing in the doorway, "and Luke's asleep. But Claire and Charlie heard it."

"Weird."

"Bloody hell, Nao. It's like a sauna in here."

"Radiator's playing silly buggers. Last night I was freezing my arse off."

"Same here," says Sharon. "No point calling the landlord, though. He'll only use the snow as an excuse not to come."

"That's pretty backwards."

"I know, but it's true. Anyway, while we're here, do you want to do a movie night soon? We figured the whole house could use some cheering up. Especially Luke."

"How about Tuesday? I know it's a wee while off, but I've got quite a lot on my plate."

"Charlie might be away," says James. "But at least Luke will be better by then. No fun watching a movie without a couple of beers."

Six

THE CENTRE OF HARTMOUTH is pretty shit for hanging out, especially on a Sunday in the middle of winter, but it beats being stuck at number thirteen all day. There's been such a weird atmosphere lately, a feeling that Sadie can't quite put her finger on. Almost as though the house is holding its breath.

Taking her glass of wine from the bar, she finds a window table in the smoking section. It's nice and warm here, and she can kill an hour or two with the book she just bought. Reading's been a great escape these past few years, a way of going into another world while the one around her fell apart.

But she just can't seem to get into it right now, which is pretty unusual. What happened to Luke is a bit of a downer, sure. And the weird goings-on in the house, like that awful smell coming out of the drains, might be annoying, but they're hardly the end of the world. And what else is there? Being blamed for poisoning everyone with that curry? Suck it up, Sades, you've dealt with way worse shit than that.

She lights a cigarette and relishes the sensation of the smoke going into her lungs. Coupled with the hit of the wine, it helps to take the edge off, and she could easily buy herself a whole bottle—single glasses are a total rip-off here—and settle in for the duration. Then again, she has lectures tomorrow, so maybe it's not the wisest of ideas.

***

The swelling around Luke's nose and eyes is now in retreat, and the whites are finally beginning to clear. It's been a bloody rough week, what with a bout of the shits and those appalling dreams of murder and mutilation—maybe a result of being concussed—but he feels like things are looking up at last.

"Hello, stranger," says Claire as he comes into the living room.

"Hey, Claire. Hey, Charlie."

"I've been keeping your spot warm for you."

"Better not have been farting there, young prince," he says with a cautious smile. "That's my prerogative."

"Look who's swallowed a dictionary," says Claire. "Are you going to join us?"

"Cup of tea first, I think."

"I'll make you one."

"It's alright, Claire. I've been on my ass all week."

"Suit yourself."

Luke heads out to the kitchen, leaving Claire and Charlie to resume their chat about his upcoming chess tournament and the teammate he's sweet on, only to come back several minutes later complaining that the milk is like cottage cheese.

"That's weird," says Claire. "Only bought it yesterday. Is the fridge working properly?"

"Well, the light comes on when you open the door," Luke replies. "Besides, it's so damn cold out there, it would hardly make a difference anyway."

***

Stanley and Naoka finish their coffee and cheesecake, then lapse into that awkward silence peculiar to people on the verge of something more than friendship. She smiles and offers a little shrug, which he mirrors before glancing over at the cafe's oversized wall clock.

"Almost three," he says. "Do you want to head back to the house?"

"Not particularly, but we probably should. I still have some reading to do for tomorrow."

"Anything I can help with?"

"Not really. It's pretty basic stuff. But thanks anyway."

They leave the cafe and make their way across the square, and as they pass the Weatherstones pub, Naoka catches sight of Sadie in the window, apparently lost in thought.

"Oh bugger," she says.

"What's wrong?"

"Sades. I don't know if she saw us."

"Who cares what she thinks? Or any of them, for that matter."

"No need to be like that. They're actually sound enough when you get to know them. Just, well, I'd rather things moved along naturally without having to answer any awkward questions."

"If you say so."

"I do, Stanley." They round the corner now, out of sight of the pub, and she reaches for his hand. "Come down and watch this movie on Tuesday night. Maybe they can start to figure it out for themselves."

***

Sharon chose entirely the wrong shoes for a trip to Lyme Street, and James can't help but tease her for it. She almost fell over a dozen times on the icy pavement walking up there, and coming back she's already had to clasp his arm twice to save herself from going head over heels.

"Easy, tiger."

"Sorry," she says, almost dropping the jumbo packet of toilet paper they just picked up at Bestmart, along with various household supplies.

"Never mind. Nearly there now anyway."

They press on along Lyme Street, the plastic bag in James's left hand threatening to cut off the blood supply to his fingers, laden as it is with washing-up liquid and bleach and toilet cleaner. And after they turn down into Cromwell Lane, the sky a shade of purplish blue, Sharon points to the house.

"Look," she says. "Ours is the only one that still has snow on the roof."

***

So then, Naoka and Stanley. That's a turn up for the books, though if Sadie thinks about it, maybe it's not that surprising. They're both nerds, for a start, and not to be cruel, but he seems like the type of guy who'd seek out a quiet little Asian girl.

Against her own wishes, sort of, she bought herself two more glasses of wine, so in total she's had a bottle anyway. Just at twice the fucking price. Which was stupid. But never mind. It's okay. She can get a taxi back to the house and go to bed early and still be fairly fresh in the morning.

Leaving the Weatherstones on floaty legs, she pauses to light another cigarette—the last in the packet, fuck—and makes for the train station at the edge town, the easiest place by far to snag a taxi. There's also a toilet there, because guaranteed she'll soon be needing another pee.

Ten minutes later she reaches the station, her breath coming out ragged and steamy in the fading daylight. And as she goes inside and passes the ticket counters en route to the toilet, she's hit with a powerful sense of foreboding. Like the one she had the night her mother decided to kiss the world goodbye. *Don't go back to the house, Sades. Just hop on the next train to anywhere, and never look back.*

Seven

The movie is of the supernatural sort, and so far it hasn't failed to disappoint. Slowly mounting levels of dread, a couple of excellent jump scares, and a heroine whose dubious choices leave most of the housemates grinding their teeth.

"Thank God Charlie's not here," says James, working his way through beer number three. "He'd be shouting his bloody head off by now."

"Bless him," says Claire, who's sharing the second sofa with Naoka and a peevish-looking Stanley. "He's too sweet and innocent to be watching things like this."

"They say it's the quiet ones you've got to watch out for."

"Shut up, James."

"Anyone for another drink?" Luke asks.

"You offering?"

"Not exactly." He lets out a long and rasping burp. "But

I'm sure one of these lovely ladies wouldn't mind."

"Cheeky bastard," says Sadie, nudging him. "Lucky for you I need to pee. Anyone else?"

"You and your bladder."

"Hit pause then, will you? I don't mind playing dogsbody, but I'm not missing half the movie."

"Alright, keep your wig on."

"Stanley, can I get you anything while I'm up?"

"I'm alright, thanks."

So out Sadie goes, heading upstairs to the bleach-smelling bathroom, where she does her business, washes her hands, and looks at herself in the mirror. Bit rough around the edges, my dear, but that's what happens when you get woken by imaginary screams at stupid o'clock in the morning.

She abandons her reflection and heads down to the kitchen for a quick cigarette. Standing just inside the back door and blowing her smoke into the blackness of the yard, she suddenly feels her hackles rise. Then the floorboards creak behind her, and she nearly jumps clean out of her skin.

"Jesus, Stanley. You almost gave me a heart attack."

"Sorry."

"…"

"Always been light on my feet."

"Like creeping fucking Jesus," she says, heart still racing. "Want one of these?"

"Prefer to roll my own."

They smoke in silence, and quickly. Though tempted to

mention seeing him with Naoka the other day, Sadie decides against it. If she were in the same boat, the last thing she'd want is an awkward conversation with someone she doesn't know that well. Better leave them to it and hope it doesn't all go to rat shit.

"We should get back," she says, flicking her cigarette butt into the yard. "Before they send out a search party."

Stanley follows her to the living room, where she hands out the beers before flopping down next to Luke. And once the recriminations about taking forever are dispensed with, the movie gets underway again.

The heroine is now conducting research into the history of her haunted home. Microfiche news clippings in the local library. Headlines about a series of brutal murders that took place there backalong. Eerie music for a nice little sense of foreboding.

"Honestly," says James, "I'd be moving out right away."

"And go where?"

"I don't know, Sharon. A hotel, a friend's house."

"That'd be the end of the movie, though, wouldn't it?" says Luke. "Sorry, dear viewer. She wised up and flogged the place to the next poor bastard."

"Bet she calls in some expert now. They'll do a spiritual cleansing of the house and everything will seem okay for a while."

"Then the evil spirit will come back with a vengeance, and things will go fucking haywire."

"I don't know why you guys bother watching," says Claire, "if you're not going to go along with it."

"Suspension of disbelief."

"Don't get him started," Luke says, sniggering. "He'll be on his soapbox for the rest of the movie. Remember that spiel about the banality of evil or whatever?"

"The what?"

"Banality, Sades. Like, we assume that evil has some grand purpose, but most of the time it's just stupid and ugly and vicious. I mean, look at—"

"Alright, James, enough."

The next scene involves, as predicted, the enlisting of an expert, in this case a local faith healer. But before she can go through the rigmarole of some cheesy cleansing ritual, the poor woman is hounded out of the house and ends up running away, panic-eyed and shrieking.

"Dream scene next," says James.

"Or bathroom mirror."

"Shut up, you two," says Sharon, twisting the cap off another bottle of wine. "You're spoiling it for the rest of us."

"I'm sure Stan and Nao don't mind. Looks like they've only got eyes for each other anyway."

Stanley's face flushes hot, and his desire to throttle Luke increases tenfold. About the only non-idiot here is Sadie, and possibly Claire, though the jury's still out on her. Fancy plonking herself between him and Nao, like some kind of porky chaperone.

"Here we go," says James. "What did I tell you?"

The heroine is now in the bathroom splashing water on her face, while behind her in the mirror the evil presence begins to manifest. And as she raises her head and starts to scream, the TV screen goes black and the lights at number thirteen go out.

"Fuck's sake."

"Oh, bloody hell."

"Can't blame my straighteners this time," says Sharon.

"Stanley?"

"And I was just beginning to enjoy myself," he says, his face now illuminated by the orange flame of his cigarette lighter. "Sadie, care to assist?"

"Can't think of anything I'd like more."

Stanley stands and fetches the torch from the drawer beneath the TV, its beam strong and sharp thanks to a brand-new set of batteries.

"Luke, James, you're not just sitting there while we do all the work," says Sadie. "Come on."

The four of them head down the hallway, following the stark white light of the torch, and when they get to the cellar door and Stanley opens it, a terrible odour comes out to meet them. Not just mildew but something altogether more unpleasant.

"Woo ooh."

"Shut the fuck up, Luke." Sadie stamps on his toes. "Go on, get in there and give him a hand."

Stanley creeps down towards the panel now, the unholy stink getting stronger with each creaking footstep.

"Bloody hell," says Luke. "Did something die down there, or what?"

"You're not helping, mate."

"Sorry, Stan."

"Bloody hell, all of them have tripped." Clicking sounds echo in the gloom as he resets the individual switches. "Okay, now for the main breaker. And the good lord said, let there be light."

A cheer erupts from the living room, but the sense of elation on the cellar stairs is very short lived, as first Luke then Stanley catch sight of what lies in wait on the dirty linoleum floor.

Eight

Charlie's eyes are wide open, his tongue lolling out almost lewdly through shriek-shaped lips. His body lies in a foetal position, back towards the staircase, neck twisted around so he appears to be gazing up at them and leering.

"Oh, fuck," Luke wheezes, backing up the stairs and falling over his own feet. "Oh, fucking hell."

Stanley retches and vomits, almost dropping the torch, and the two of them scramble towards the yellow light of the hallway, where James and Sadie wait in stunned confusion.

"What is it?" James asks, his voice high and querulous.

"Charlie. It's fucking Charlie."

Stanley shuts the cellar door and leans with his back against it, still trying to process what he's just seen. His mouth is foul with vomit, and his entire body is shaking.

"What do you mean?" Sadie asks. "He's not even here."

"It's fucking Charlie, alright. Unless me and Stan are

both hallucinating."

"What's going on?" Sharon comes out to the hallway, tailed by Claire and Naoka.

"Charlie's in the cellar."

"What do you mean? Charlie's away with the chess team."

"No, he's not," says Stanley, wiping the last of the vomit from his mouth with the back of his hand. "He's lying on the cellar floor, as dead as a doornail."

"What?" says Claire. "He can't be."

"Take a look for yourself." Stanley steps away from the cellar door and gestures at it limply.

"Someone should call an ambulance."

"What good would that do?" Luke asks. "If he's dead?"

"I knew I heard a scream last night."

"Me too, Sades," says Sharon. "Do you think it was him?"

"He can't be dead." Claire's voice is rising now, on the verge of hysterical. "He can't be. Someone go and check. It must be a mistake."

But a mistake it most certainly is not, proven beyond doubt when Sadie gets up the gumption to open the cellar door and peer down into the darkness. With the aid of the torch and the hallway light behind her, she can just make out Charlie's stricken form, his dead eyes glinting up at her almost mockingly.

***

When the police arrive, followed in short order by an ambulance crew, they venture down and fit the lightbulb Stanley has borrowed from the office. The cellar is unremarkable, a largely empty space with several old pieces of furniture and some decorating supplies, the only noteworthy feature, of course, being a dead teenager lying in a puddle of his own mess.

A cursory survey reveals no obvious cause of death—no apparent signs of a fall—and initial statements taken from the lad's housemates give no suggestion of foul play. A very sad, yet not improbable, case of massive heart failure by the looks of it. Some might go as far as to say frightened to death, but who in their right mind would put that on a report?

"The coroner is sending someone now to collect the body," the male officer says to a shivering Sadie on the front path. "And we might ask you to come to the station if our investigation requires it."

"Of course."

"Just to remind you, I'm Constable Clement," he says, then nods to his partner as she squeezes past with the departing ambulance crew. "And my colleague is Constable White."

"Okay, got it."

"Keep out of the cellar for now, please, as it constitutes a crime scene until we can confirm otherwise."

"No fear of that," says Sadie. "You'd have to pay me a million pounds."

And twenty minutes later, once Charlie's stiff and

crooked body has been carted away, the two officers depart from number thirteen, leaving its inhabitants to lie awake most of the night in varying states of misery and confusion.

Nine

No one attends lectures on Wednesday, not even Stanley. Last night's horrors, not to mention the overall lack of sleep, have rendered the housemates almost catatonic. And as morning bleeds into afternoon, they filter into the living room, unconsciously taking their places from the night before, save for Naoka bagging the middle spot beside Stanley.

"I can't believe it." Claire blows her nose into a wad of tissue. "We had a lovely little lunch in the refectory on Monday, and now he's gone."

"What about his parents?" Sharon asks.

"The police will let them know," says Sadie. "And I suppose they'll have to come and get his stuff sooner or later."

"Do you think we should pack it up for them?"

"I'd leave well alone," says Luke. "I mean, what if they discover he was on drugs or something and want to search his room?"

"Oh, that's charming, that is."

"Easy, Claire."

"No, Sharon. His first concern is always for himself. Not that it would be heartbreaking to pack up his poor dead housemate's things. No. He's only worried he might get a slap on the wrist if the police need to conduct a search."

"Come on," says Stanley. "That's hardly fair."

"What the hell would you know about it, Mr Penthouse? Come in here once in a blue moon and think you can tell any of us what's fair or not?"

"That's enough, Claire," says Sadie. "Lashing out is just making a bad situation even worse. You think Charlie would be impressed to see you laying into Luke and Stanley?"

"Don't you dare use his name against me like that." Claire gets to her feet and storms to the door. "Don't you fucking dare."

And then she's gone, her footsteps pounding up the stairs, the housemates looking at one another in bemusement.

"Christ on a bike."

"You can say that again, James my boy."

"I'll check on her in a minute," says Sharon. "Sorry about that, Stanley."

"It's understandable I suppose, given the situation. I take it they were close."

"Her more than him, I think," says Sadie. "Charlie was pretty much everyone's best friend."

***

Around half past three, a tacit decision is made to decamp to the kitchen and polish off last night's booze. And if push comes to shove, to purchase more until the jagged edges of the day are a little more rounded. Sharon and Naoka will join them in a while, if and when things are peachier with Claire.

"Thought you were teetotal, Stan."

"More or less, Luke. But I make the odd exception."

"Why?"

"Why make an exception? Or why am I more or less teetotal?"

"Either. Both."

"Well the first one's fairly obvious, but the reason I don't partake that often is I'm not very good at stopping."

"Like, alcoholic?"

"Not really. I can go without it easily enough, I just tend to drink myself under the table when I do."

"Well, don't let us stop you," says James. "Can I pinch a smoke, by the way?"

Stanley pries open his tobacco tin, which contains a handful of pre-rolled efforts, and passes one over. Then he and James go to the back door and light up.

"What I want to know," says Luke from the table, "is what the fuck was he even doing in the cellar?"

"Maybe he was sleepwalking," says Sadie, pouring herself another glass of wine. "No sane person would ever go down there of their own accord."

"Can't imagine what his folks must be going through."

"Well, Stan, they're kind of weird if you ask me," says Luke. "Send him to some shitty old student house in the back of beyond and leave him to fend for himself. He'd have been better off at Oxford or something."

"Maybe they're not as wealthy as you think," says Sadie. "A lot of these well-to-do families are actually on the bones of their ass."

"I guess."

"Hey, Nao. Where's Sharon?"

"She'll be down in a minute, Sades," she says, pulling up a chair. "Pour us a wee drink then."

"How are things with Claire?" Stanley flicks his roll-up away and comes back to the table.

"Better, I think."

"Talk about losing the plot," says James from the doorway.

"Go easy on her, will you? If anything, her reaction is more appropriate than any of ours."

"Alright, sorry."

"Anyway, she's going to have a bath." Naoka takes a sip of her wine. "Then come down later if she's feeling up to it."

"Looks like we're all peeing on the second floor then."

"You always pee on the floor anyway, Luke."

"So you're the culprit," says Stanley, cocking an eyebrow. "Any chance of another beer?"

***

Claire gazes at her tear-streaked face in the mirror while the bathtub fills the room with billows of steam. Poor old Charlie. Such a gentle soul. If only there was something she could have done.

"Should've been you," she mutters to her reflection. "No one would cry over a fat piece of shit like you."

And hearing the words aloud, they seem to ring horribly true. She is a fat piece of shit, and a terrible friend to boot. Sades had it right. Using Charlie's death to lash out at everyone else. What kind of friend would dream of doing such a thing?

"Fat piece of worthless shit," she says to the mirror, her eyes going wide, her breath rising up thick and foul from her disgusting dung heap of a stomach. "No one's going to cry over you. Might as well take Luke's shitty razor there and put yourself out of your misery."

And with dreadful, almost automatic focus, she takes it from the soap dish and begins to break it apart. The handle comes off first and rattles into the sink, then she twists and bends the head, the blade coming free and biting into her fingers.

"Don't worry, little piggy," she says in a voice not quite her own. "The pain won't last for long."

Now she crosses to the bathtub, already half full and piping hot, and steps into it, knowing the water is scalding her feet yet somehow enjoying the sensation. Lowering herself into the steaming water, she leans forwards and turns off the tap before lying back and holding the razor blade aloft.

"Let's do it right, piggy chops," she says. "Not across but along, and nice and deep."

The first cut brings a sense of relief, like peeing when you've been holding it for hours. And the second brings more relief still, the blood flowing freely now from the bright pink meat of her arms. She changes hands and starts on the other side, almost taking pride in the slow, deliberate parting of her veins.

"This little piggy went to market, and you know what market means, don't you? She wasn't going shopping, you silly girl. No, no, no. She was going to be sold and taken to slaughter, and her plump little throat was going to be opened, just like so."

And now she smiles, and a curious smile it is, as she holds the blade aloft again, then brings it, hand trembling, towards her throat. No one will cry over a fat piece of worthless shit like her, except maybe Charlie, and she'll be seeing him soon enough.

Ten

As one might expect, the police raised an eyebrow or two about Claire's very emphatic death, but in the end it all made reasonable sense. Distraught and unstable in the aftermath of a close friend's tragic passing. And in the following days, two sets of shattered parents come to collect their children's belongings from number thirteen, Charlie's yesterday evening and Claire's this afternoon.

"Better get started," says her father. "Would someone mind..."

"Of course." Sharon ushers him out of the living room, leaving a dispirited-looking James alone with Claire's mother on the main sofa. "This way."

"I'm so sorry."

"Thank you, love," she says quietly.

"Can I get you anything?"

"No, it's alright. I'll be drowning in tea if I'm not careful."

That really would be something, he thinks, almost laughing out loud. Imagine the headlines. In wake of fat-assed daughter's blood bath, fat-assed mother drowns in vat of tea. Fat-assed father put on suicide watch. Only, her father is as thin as a rake, so that last part doesn't really work. Besides, what a cruel thing to imagine.

"... happy here?"

"Um, sorry, what was that?"

"I was just wondering if Claire was happy here."

"Oh, yes." Despite being a gluttonous slut who couldn't stop filling her filthy cakehole. "Pretty much, I'd say."

"She spoke well of all of you. Especially Charlie."

Well, he was the only one polite enough to listen to her drivel, wasn't he, you daft cow? Maybe if you'd raised her better, she wouldn't have ended up cutting herself to ribbons.

"... long journey back."

"Yes, of course."

"Shouldn't be too bad," she says, twitching her nose as if smelling something offensive. "If we can get on the road by three."

"Mmm hmm."

"..."

What on earth is going on with these awful thoughts? And why the compulsion to say them out loud? It feels as though someone else is behind his wheel and is trying to drive him off the nearest cliff. But Claire really was a fat piece of shit, wasn't she? And her mother doesn't appear to be much better. Go on, tell her what a fat fucking waste of space her daughter was, and how everyone's secretly glad she killed herself.

"... feeling alright?"

"Sorry?"

"You seemed to have drifted off for a moment."

"Hardly a surprise, is it? You're just as fucking tedious as your daughter."

"Hi, folks," says Sharon, coming into the room. "Can I offer anyone a cup of tea?"

James blinks several times, takes in the horrified expression on the face of Claire's mother, then slumps into the corduroy confines of the sofa, wishing it would swallow him up.

Eleven

"There's something wrong with the house." Luke skews his shot and pots one of Sadie's yellows. "I mean, really wrong."

"Yep," says James from his seat at the table behind them. "It's like the place is cursed."

"First Charlie, then Claire."

"This curse extend to your pool-playing skills as well?" asks Sadie, moving the white behind the line.

"You know what I'm talking about."

And the fact of the matter is, Sadie does know what Luke's talking about. Not just the loss of their friends—and God knows Claire's suicide has stirred up some pretty gnarly feelings—but all the other weirdness. The noises in the night, the rapid changes in temperature, the food going bad in the fridge. And more than anything, the almost palpable sense of dread running through the place like the words in a stick of Hartmouth rock.

"I was thinking," says Luke.

"Makes a change."

"Thank you, my boy. But seriously, it does feel like the house is cursed. You don't suppose…"

"That what happened in the graveyard has something to do with it?"

"Well," says Sadie, wanting to scoff at the idea but unable to do so. "I'd be lying if I said it hasn't crossed my mind."

"…"

"It's ridiculous, though, isn't it? Just a stupid bit of horror movie lore."

But now that the words are out there, the three of them begin to entertain the notion. The house was fine before Luke's accident, and it's been anything but fine ever since. What harm could a little research do? They could start with a trip to the scene of the crime, and if nothing else, it will give them a sense of agency.

***

Stanley and Naoka lie partly entwined in his bed, looking up at the sloping ceiling as wintry sunlight comes in from the terrace. Maybe a touch too soon, she thinks, but it was going to come anyway, or not come, as the case may be. The sound of Sharon's music drifts up the staircase, and all seems as well with the world as it can be, given recent events.

"That doesn't usually happen."

"Don't fret about it, Stan the man."

"Oh, don't," he says with a meek laugh. "The last thing I want to be thinking about is Luke."

"Aye, right enough."

"..."

"Just so you know, by the way, I won't be kipping here overnight. Don't take it personally, this is all going along just fine, but I think we should keep a few boundaries for now."

Stanley turns his head to face her. "Fair enough. Though I can't say I won't be tempted to pay you a visit now and then."

"I think that might be alright," she says as he leans in to kiss her. "But don't expect me to return the favour. I'd sooner shit in my hands and clap than go creeping around this place in the middle of the night. Especially with all that's gone on."

"Shit in your hands and clap?"

"That'll be Sades rubbing off on me, I suppose. But seriously, I'm not sold on the idea of sticking around much longer."

Can't blame her for that, he thinks. None of the others are keen on staying either, Stanley included, but they've agreed to wait a month or two before deciding whether or not to jump ship. Spring's not all that far away, and the longer days and warmer weather might paint things in a slightly better light.

"I'm famished," says Naoka. "Do you fancy a bit of

brekkie?"

"Bit late for that. It's almost one o'clock."

"Well, lunch then."

"Maybe we can try again first," he says, giving her a hopeful smile and reaching beneath the covers.

"Maybe indeed," she replies, enjoying the warmth of his tentative touch. "But not too long, eh? I wasn't kidding about being famished."

***

Admirable restraint was shown in the Red Lion, and the three housemates arrive at the graveyard relatively sober. The sky has a washed out look to it, white-grey cloud against a backdrop of pale, dirty blue.

"Act natural," says Luke as they pass a grave digger, or whoever it is that carries long-handled tools around a graveyard on a Tuesday afternoon. "Don't want to get asked to leave before we've checked out the, well, you know…"

They reach and pass the chapel, Sadie noting with an internal roll of the eyes the spot where she took a pee that fateful night. And she wonders, just for a moment, what her life would be like without the demon drink, which always seems to give with one hand and take with the other.

"This way, right?" James asks.

"I think so. It all looks different in the daylight."

"Profound insight there, Luke."

"Thank you, James my boy," he says lightheartedly, despite feeling anything but. "Yeah, I'm pretty sure this is the way."

They head south, the ground gently sloping down towards an older, more overgrown section of the graveyard, a lichen-covered angel here, a broken headstone there. And now, yes, over there in the corner. That's the place.

Daylight now lays bare what darkness had obscured. The fence in this corner has collapsed completely, stray posts and palings jutting here and there through a snarl of brambles and weeds. And right in the back there, like a solitary, rotten tooth, is the gravestone in question.

"I'll be honest," says Luke. "I really don't want to go in there again."

"Well, I'm not."

"For fuck's sake," says Sadie. "Out of the way then, boys."

"..."

Smaller and more agile than Luke, she makes a fairly easy job of it, only catching herself a couple of times on the tangled matrix of thorns.

"Can you see anything?"

"I think these are splashes of blood, but it's hard to tell. Plenty of rain and snow these past few weeks."

"Is that it? No name or…"

"No, looks like just the date. Wonder why that is."

"Yeah, weird."

"One thing, though," she says, a chill going up the backs

of her legs. "Judging by the position of these posts, it's actually outside the graveyard. Wouldn't that be unconsecrated ground?"

Twelve

Out of all the remaining housemates, Sharon is the only one to have taken up the university's offer of counselling. And it's not so much that she feels she needs it but that she considers it a way of honouring Charlie and Claire. Otherwise, well, it almost seems like no one's taken their passing seriously.

"And how are the others doing?" asks the counsellor, a woman in her late forties with a knitted cardigan and patent leather ankle boots.

"Sadie's been a bit quiet, understandably I guess, but mostly they've just been drinking."

"Well, that won't do them any favours in the long run."

"Of course." Sharon glances at one of the many motivational posters lining the walls of the office. "But it's good for getting to sleep."

"And for waking up at four in the morning feeling rotten."

"True," she says with a rueful smile. "It does end up making you feel worse."

"How about your lectures? Are you keeping on top of things?"

"Catching up slowly. They've given us extensions."

"And rightly so. Try to make use of them if you can. You might find focusing on your studies helps keep your mind off things."

"Is that what I'm supposed to be doing?"

"There's a difference between suppressing our troubles and setting them to one side."

"…"

"Anyway, I think that's us for today. Same time next week?"

"Yes, please."

"And do consider that journal I mentioned. Any feelings that arise, any recurring thoughts or dreams. It's good to get them out of the head and onto the page."

Not the dreams, thinks Sharon as she leaves the office and crosses the quad to the campus library, where she's arranged to meet up with Sadie and the boys. Peeling the skin from Luke's roasted corpse and popping it in her mouth like pork crackling? Some things just should not be written down.

***

On the other side of town, Stanley and Naoka arrive at

the central library, where they can make use of the public volumes and the archives. The weather is bright and sunny for a change, but still bitterly cold, and they're glad of the warmth as they stroll through the reception area and into the library main.

"Where should we start?" Naoka asks.

"Local history, maybe. Find what we can, then enquire at the desk if we need anything more."

"Right you are, then."

Stanley allows her to lead the way, his mood somewhere between carefree and serious. Though a large part of him wants to dismiss the whole thing as a wild goose chase, a smaller part is genuinely intrigued. Besides, as harebrained as it all seems, there's no denying that something isn't right at the house. A sort of collective hysteria it may be, but he can't dismiss what he's been seeing with his own two eyes.

They reach the local history section, and Stanley leaves her to find what she can while he hunts for books on witchcraft and the occult, joining her ten minutes later at one of the circular tables by the far wall.

"This is all there was," says Naoka. "*A History of South West England* and *Hartmouth Through the Centuries*."

"Let's start with those then, and take a look at mine after."

"Right enough, captain."

"Really?"

"Beam us up, will you?"

It turns out that the Hartmouth book contains little of interest, just a passing mention of witchcraft in the seventeenth century, but the second book is far more illuminating. Occult practices did take place in the region, and so-called witches were either hanged or, on rare occasions, burned at the stake.

"Looks like plain old Satanism then," says Naoka. "You have to wonder what these folks got out of it. I mean, considering the punishment if you were caught, you'd want a pretty amazing payoff."

"Says here the practitioner would have entered into a contract with the devil or demon, agreeing to perform certain actions in return for secret knowledge, power, wealth, or the ability to harm or dominate others."

Moving now to Stanley's haul of books, which includes *A Compendium of Witchcraft* and *On the Occult*, they find themselves going down a very dark and unseemly rabbit hole. The rites and acts these people would partake in range from the strange and silly to the downright disgusting and depraved.

"Some rituals would require human or blood sacrifice, with certain body parts, such as the liver, heart, and genitals, offered up by way of payment." Stanley skims down a few lines. "The process of removing these parts would often happen while the victim was still alive."

"Dear God, can you imagine the pain and terror of getting carved open like that? Of being awake through the whole thing?"

"With any luck you'd pass out," he says with a shudder, then nods at the book in her hands. "Anything about how these bastards were buried after execution?"

"Hang on," she says, turning the page. "Yeah, right here. Often they were placed in unmarked graves on unconsecrated ground."

"Well, our mystery man, or woman, has a gravestone."

"I guess there's an exception to every rule."

"True," he says.

"And look at this."

"It was believed that their spirits would remain forever in torment and could worry the living—odd choice of word that, like dogs worrying sheep—should their remains be interfered with."

"I'd say old Luke did just that, wouldn't you?"

"Bleeding all over a gravesite during a lunar eclipse?" Stanley raises an eyebrow archly. "Well, maybe just a little."

***

Unbeknown to Sadie and the others, the information they've found at the campus library adds little to what Stanley and Naoka have learned so far. But a trawl of the internet may yet yield something useful.

"Oh, look, he's being done for sexual assault."

"Who?" asks Sharon, two computers along from Luke.

"Marshman."

"Always knew he was a bit dodgy."

"Come on, guys," says Sadie. "Remember what we're here for."

"Alright, calm down."

"As if telling someone to calm down ever worked."

More adept than the others when it comes to internet searches, James has already found various sites of interest. He opens each to produce a line of four tabs across the top of his screen. The first he reads more closely and discounts, same story with the second, but the third has information about several covens in the area.

"Hey, take a look at this."

"Hartmouth has its own dark history," Sadie reads. "In the late 1660s, a particularly heinous coven had its wicked way with the local populace. Rumour has it that their leader, a local slaughterman, would cut off the victim's eyelids as part of the rite."

"Christ on a bike," says Sharon.

"In a Panzer tank, more like."

"Thanks, Luke."

"This is only a dot org site, though," says James. "So we have to take it with a pinch of salt. There's no names or specific dates, and look at the author."

"Clint Treboner."

"Thought you'd like that one, mate."

"Who doesn't enjoy a good boner, my boy?"

"What about that fourth tab?" Sadie asks. "Anything more?"

James opens it and starts to read, but there's nothing beyond what they've already learned, so they curtail their search and leave the library. It's almost half past three now, and they've arranged to catch up with Stanley and Naoka back at the house at dinner time. Hopefully they've discovered something useful and not just spent the entire afternoon banging.

Thirteen

"The other day, when Claire's dad was upstairs getting her stuff and her mum was in here with me, I had this overwhelming urge to say horrible things to her. Like how we all hated Claire and were glad she'd killed herself."

"Fucking hell, James my boy."

"I know. Believe me, I know. And the thing is, I've had intrusive thoughts before—I expect we all have—but I've never actually blurted them out."

"Maybe it's part of the grieving process."

"I don't think insulting the poor woman is part of any process, Sharon."

"Well, how can you be so sure?"

"Come on," says James, whose idea it was to share everything they've experienced in the past few weeks. "We're not trying to cast doubt on each other here."

"Alright, sorry."

"And seriously, don't hold anything back. How many

horror movies have you watched where the characters see the weirdest shit and keep it to themselves?"

"I almost jammed my fingers in the toaster," says Luke, deciding this is a better thing to discuss than the visions of pleasuring himself with Naoka's severed head.

"Oh, I've nearly done that myself a few times."

"No, Sharon, not by accident. I literally stood there rinsing my plate and started thinking how great it would be to stick my fingers in and fry myself."

The front door comes open now, followed by footsteps in the hallway, and the housemates correctly assume that it's Stanley and Naoka. After a pause, no doubt to swap a little spit, the two of them enter the living room.

"Alright, guys?"

"Hey, Stan," says Luke. "Hey, Nao. How did you get on?"

"Found out a few things," says Stanley. "But I've been thinking, if there really is a presence in the house, maybe we'd be better off discussing it elsewhere."

"Well, I'm not going up the Red Lion again," says Sadie, who up until now has been lost in thought. "Much as I'd love to get pissed again, I think a clear mind is in order."

"How about the chippy?" says Naoka. "It's usually quiet enough on a weekday night, and I could murder a bit of cod and a pickled egg."

***

Lyme Street's aptly named Pride of Plaice serves some of the best fish and chips in town, and being away from the main tourist spots, the prices are reasonable. Set off from the counter is an eating area with a handful of plastic tables. And it is here, beneath harsh fluorescent lighting, that the housemates are now convened.

"We didn't find a name," says James, dipping a soggy chip into a pot of curry sauce. "But we did find an article about some psychotic coven leader."

"Clint Treboner."

"Very menacing," says Naoka.

"That's the guy who wrote the article."

"I know, Sades. Just couldn't resist."

"We didn't find a name either," says Stanley. "But there was something in the records about this coven."

"Did it mention the eyes?"

"Apparently the leader," says Sharon, "if that's what they call them, used to slice off the victims' eyelids. To stop them from looking away, I guess."

"Warlock? Master of witchery?"

"Maybe high priest," Stanley suggests to Luke. "And no, nothing about that, appalling as it sounds. Just that the members were rounded up, tried, and hanged."

"No mention of where this guy was buried?"

"No, Sadie, but I think we can make an educated guess."

"Okay." She pushes away the remains of her battered sausage and chips. "Anything else?"

"Not really," says Naoka. "But it would've been far better for everyone if they'd burned the bastard. At least with fire the evil gets purified."

"Well, even if that is true, we can hardly go digging him up and setting things straight, can we?"

"Or burning the house down."

"Bloody tempting, my boy."

"Well," says Sadie, "we do need some kind of plan, and preferably one that won't get us arrested."

The conversation now turns to what James calls the 'expert issue'. Horror movies might supply a handy host of helpful spiritualists and exorcists, but this is the real world.

"There's a tarot guy by the seafront."

"Snake oil salesman," says Sadie. "I read a story about him in the *Herald* a while back."

"We could look online."

"Already," says Stanley. "Nothing much doing."

"I hate to say it then, but how about a priest? There's a church at the end of Outfield Road. No idea what brand of Christianity."

"Denomination, James. It's Church of England, that one. Good old home-baked Protestantism."

"So..."

"So I reckon it's worth a go. Thing is, how much of this are we going to tell them? A proper exorcism might require an investigation, and even if they do take us seriously, it could be weeks before they actually send someone."

"Fuck that," says Luke. "We can't afford to wait that long."

"Exactly."

After a little back and forth, a decision is made to enquire at the church about getting number thirteen blessed. According to Stanley, it's a fairly common thing, especially for new homeowners and recent converts. So why not for people who've had a couple of horrific deaths at their house? And the beauty of it is they won't have to spill the beans on their graveyard antics or run the risk of being laughed out of the building.

"Agreed then," says Sadie. "Nao and Stanley will go up there tomorrow."

"You could arrange your wedding while you're at it."

"Shut up, Luke."

***

The mid-February wind blows cold as the housemates head along Lyme Street, stopping off for powdered milk, cigarettes, and beers for Luke and James, neither of whom have any intention of staying completely sober.

"Before you got back earlier," Sharon says to Naoka as they round the corner and start down Cromwell Lane, "we were talking about any other weird stuff we'd experienced."

"Weirder than what's already gone on?"

"Like, personally."

"Well, I keep dreaming of all kinds of terrible stuff, some of it far too gross to even talk about."

"Me too," says Sadie, falling back to join them now as the boys push ahead. "It's like this thing's trying to break our spirits."

"Well, it's working," says Sharon, voice faltering. "I'm afraid to close my eyes these days."

Sadie puts an arm around her. "Hang in there. We won't let this bastard beat us."

"..."

"Actually," says Naoka, "something weird did happen the other day. I was out on Stanley's terrace, copping a view of the street, and I had the sudden urge to jump."

"That thing's a deathtrap."

"What stopped you?" Sadie asks.

"Oh, bloody hell..."

Joining the others outside number thirteen, they see that every light in the house is on and every window is open. And as they unlock the door and venture inside, Naoka's music starts blasting out full tilt. *Gonna slice you and dice you, little piggy, gonna slice you and dice you...*

Fourteen

Perhaps it was the recent newspaper stories that convinced the priest to take Stanley and Naoka seriously, but either way, it turns out she's more than willing to come and bless the house tomorrow morning. And with some positive news at last, plus no further incidents in the wake of yesterday's death metal fest, the housemates head to bed on Thursday night feeling just a little lighter.

For Sadie, however, sleep is slow to come, and when it does arrive, at long last, it falls over her like a smothering hand pushing her down into the void. Worse still, it feels like only moments before she's wide awake again, sitting bolt upright and unblinking in the darkness.

Her mouth is dry and sour, and when she catches a whiff of her breath, she almost vomits on the spot. Dear God, she really needs to sort this out, and with something stronger than toothpaste or mouthwash. Something purgative is in order, and lucky for her, she knows exactly where to find it. So she climbs out of bed and creeps downstairs.

When she reaches the ground floor, she heads to the kitchen, not bothering to switch the light on, and opens the cupboard beneath the kitchen sink. The bleach might do the trick, or the oven cleaner, but somewhere in the cluttered darkness is something even better.

When her hand finally alights on the bottle of drain unblocker, she fetches a cup and fills it to the brim. And now she realises that she's crying, a feeling of despair weighing down upon her at the sheer hopelessness of life and all its petty struggles.

And yet as much as she wants to knock back this killer concoction, just as her mother once did with a handful of benzos, she's also aware that she'd never dream of taking her own life. Not after seeing what suicide does to those left behind. To her sister, to her grandparents, to her.

She tries to blink and can't. Tries to cry out and can't. Tries to pour the cup down the sink and can't. All she can do is stand here, tears coursing down her cheeks, and raise the cup almost willingly to her lips. It smells so noxious, so caustic, and she knows it will ravage her mouth and throat as it burns its way down to her stomach. And then the kitchen light snaps on, and Luke's voice comes to her, far away at first but growing more insistent.

"You scared the shit out of me, Sades," he says, pushing the cup away from her face and peering into it. "And what in the holy fuck is this?"

Fifteen

And so it is that on Friday morning at ten o'clock sharp, the Reverend Jennifer Blake arrives on the doorstep with a winning smile and something resembling a Gladstone bag.

"Thanks for coming," says Sharon, leading her into the recently tidied living room, where the others are sitting in anticipation, none more so than Sadie, who remains badly shaken from last night's near miss. "Would you like a cup of tea?"

"I'll pass on that, thank you. The old bladder isn't what it used to be."

"Please, have a seat," says James, who has relinquished his armchair in honour of the eagerly awaited guest. "Are you sure we can't get you anything?"

"No, thank you, my lovely."

When the introductions are dispensed with, the reverend gives a brief rundown of the process, which is basically the anointing of each door and window within the house, accompanied by a blessing.

"No holy water?" Luke asks.

"I'll be using a simple oil, but really, it's the words and the intention that hold the power. We'll begin and conclude with a verse from Joshua."

And so the thing gets underway. The reverend opens her bag and retrieves a Bible and a small glass bottle of oil, then reads a short passage while the housemates sit in respectful silence. Then she stands and asks someone to lead the way, a duty that falls to Naoka.

"Alright then, why don't we work from top to bottom?"

"Sounds good to me," says Stanley, tagging along with the remaining housemates in solemn pursuit.

"Do you need to go into the rooms? Mine's a bit of a mess."

"If your room has a window, which I assume it does, then yes. But don't worry, my lovely. I'm not here on an inspection."

"Thank Christ for that," says Luke.

"Indeed. Now, let's have at it, shall we?"

They start in Stanley's penthouse, the reverend tracing a cross on the terrace window and door with an oil-dipped finger and reciting a simple blessing. Then she repeats the process with the internal door, and they head down to Naoka's room then Luke's, which features several iffy-looking socks and any number of empty beer cans.

During the blessing of the first-floor bathroom, smelling as dreadful as ever, one of the doors downstairs makes a brief rattling noise, but the reverend's shrug and beatific smile allay their fears.

"One more floor to go," she says, following Naoka downstairs and out to the kitchen. "My goodness, it's chilly in here, isn't it?"

"Heating's a bit temperamental," says Stanley. "We'll be glad when the winter's over, that's for sure."

"No doubt you will, my lovely."

After the kitchen comes the cellar door, and everyone holds their breath.

"In the name of Our Lord Jesus Christ," the reverend intones, her practised finger running smoothly across the paintwork, "we ask for Your joy and peace to inhabit this space."

And if any of the housemates were expecting fireworks, which truth be told was all of them, they're sorely disappointed. No shake, no rattle, and no demonic moaning. Nothing but a cool and blessed silence. And when the remaining doors and windows are done, they gather in the living room, where the reverend once again reads a verse before returning the oil and Bible to her bag.

"So, it's finished?" Luke asks.

"It is indeed, my lovely. Now, two things before I make a move. First, I'm all too aware of the tragedy you've experienced in this house. Grief and stress have a way of manifesting all sorts of unpleasantness, and I would advise you to focus on living as well as you can. A visit or two to the church wouldn't go amiss, either. And please, do your best to foster some positivity. Go out and socialise, have some fun together. A blessing cleanses a home, but it's up to all of you to keep it that way."

Almost in unison, the housemates murmur their agreement.

"What was the second thing?" Sadie asks.

"Oh, yes. Would you mind if I used your bathroom?"

"Of course."

"I'll find my own way," she says, standing and making for the door. "Won't be a minute."

The sounds of her footsteps recede upstairs, and the housemates hear the bathroom door open and close. Then a minute or so later, a short sharp shriek pierces the silence.

"Fucking hell," says Luke, jumping to his feet and racing upstairs with James and Stanley in tow. And he's about to try the door handle when the reverend steps out.

"I know they're the Good Lord's creatures as well," she says, her face a livid shade of pink. "But spiders scare the living daylights out of me."

Sixteen

Taking seriously the reverend's advice to do something positive with their time, the six housemates depart from number thirteen on a bright and breezy Sunday morning. It's been a long while since any of them went to the seafront, and though the weather remains as cold as charity, they can still have a little fun. Grab a bite to eat at the lido cafe, then take it from there.

"Love me a student card," says Luke, ever pleased to receive a discount for bus travel. "Shame I can't use it for beer."

"Have you tried getting on your knees?"

"Fuck off, Sades."

"Look alive, folks," says Naoka. "This is our stop."

They disembark at the midway point of Riviera Road, only a stone's throw from the lido. A low wall runs parallel to the pavement, with several openings to a series of paths and steps leading all the way down to the bay below, as well as to the lido entrance. From way up here the thing is quite a sight, a huge blue and white wedding cake with one large pool and several smaller ones for the children.

"When do they fill it?" James asks. "Be ideal to have a swim before heading home for the summer."

"Looks like some people can't wait." Stanley points down to a broad concrete landing, where several swimmers are getting ready to take the plunge. "Rather them than me."

"My mum used to be big into sea swimming," says Luke. "Good for the heart, apparently."

"Think it would stop mine dead," says Naoka, recalling trips to the Banffshire coast before her family moved to London.

They walk down and across to the cafe, which sits just above the lido and has a view of the entire bay, and order coffees and toasted sandwiches. Then they find a table and make themselves comfortable, glad to be out of the cold for a while.

"This is nice," says Sharon.

"I had a teacher who wouldn't let us use the word nice. Said it was the most overused and underwhelming adjective in the English language."

"That's nice, James."

"Nice of you to say so, Sharon."

After a while, the conversation drifts towards the inevitable. No one really wants to break the ice and say how much better things have been in the house, as though afraid of jinxing it. But break the ice they eventually do, with Sadie mentioning how her radiator is working properly at last.

"Mine too," says Sharon.

"And the drains have stopped smelling like roadkill."

"Thanks, Luke. I'm trying to eat here."

"Sorry." He flashes Naoka a grin. "But it's true, no?"

"Aye, right enough."

"Two solid nights of sleep," says Stanley. "And not a nightmare to be had."

"I think the less we say about those, the better. Least said soonest mended, as my nan likes to say."

"Quite right, Sades."

"Okay, so what shall we do after this?" Sharon asks. "Part of me wants to crack open a bottle of wine and celebrate."

"Let's wait until midweek, eh? There's that audit thing on Thursday, so no lectures."

"Are you feeling alright, Luke?"

"Yeah. I mean, it just feels a bit soon to be really going for it."

Almost chastened by this rare moment of wisdom, they decide to swing by the penny arcade then see how they feel afterwards. Maybe catch a movie, maybe take a look around whatever shops are open in the town centre.

They stroll back along Riviera Road, down to the little harbour with its smattering of fishing boats, and head into the arcade. Out of season, there aren't many people around, giving them free rein of the sliding trays and one-arm bandits.

"Cha-ching," cries Luke, a rush of coins sliding noisily into the collection slot. "Told you I was going to clean up."

"Must be at least three quid there." Sadie laughs. "Don't spend it all at once."

Stanley and Naoka have a crack at one of the older amusements, little mechanised horses and jockeys racing along narrow tracks, and James joins Sharon over at the fruit machines.

"Are you any good at these?" he asks.

"Not bad. My parents used to run a pub when I was younger."

"I always end up losing the lot."

"Never risk what you can't afford to lose," she says, her eyes smiling. "Unless it's in matters of the heart, of course."

"Then what?"

"Then you go for broke."

And as though on cue, the tumblers line up in the little window before her, three golden jackpot signs. The lights start flashing and a merry tune erupts, the digital display counting up from a solitary pound to fifty one.

"Fucking hell," Luke calls across, almost broke already. "Looks like dinner's on you two."

***

Having left before they bankrupted themselves, or in Sharon's case the arcade owner, they enjoyed an ice cream by the harbourside before heading into town for another round of coffees. And after a stroll around Lamprey Park they headed back home, picking up a couple of pizzas on the way, courtesy of Sharon.

Feeling the wholesome sort of weariness that only comes from a good day out, they sit together now in the living room until Stanley excuses himself on the pretext of finishing an assignment. And within an hour, both Naoka and Sharon have also made their way upstairs.

"Well, it's too early for me to turn in just yet."

"I'll probably give it another hour, mate," says James. "But there's got to be something better to watch than this."

"Are you telling me," Sadie winks, "that you don't appreciate middle-class housewives searching their attics for antiques?"

"Wonder if there's any in the attic of this place."

"Pretty sure the attic is Stanley's bedroom, Luke."

"Indeed, my boy. Just checking to see if you were paying attention."

"I'm going for a smoke," says Sadie. "See if you can find something decent to watch, and that doesn't include any form of sports."

"Right you are, ginger ninja."

She goes out to the back door and takes a pack of cigarettes from her pocket, and the yard is so dark that she doesn't notice the cat until it's right in front of her. One of the largest she's ever seen, black as the night with impish blue eyes.

"Hello, boy," she says. "Would you like a saucer of

milk?"

The cat looks up and pokes out a bright red tongue, which she assumes means yes. She goes to the cupboard and fetches a saucer, then takes the milk from the fridge, heart fluttering a little as she begins to pour. What if it's curdled again? What if this is all just a temporary reprieve? But it comes out just fine, and she turns to the cat with a smile, only to find it gone.

"Guys," she says, returning to the living room, cigarette not yet smoked. "Have you ever seen a black cat hanging around the yard?"

"A black cat?"

"Yeah, Luke. Really big, with bright blue eyes."

"Never seen it in my life. Maybe it's the evil spirit returned in another form."

"You wanker," she says.

He bursts into a peal of laughter, long and loud, and it's the first time in weeks that she's seen him so relaxed.

"Really, though, have you?"

"All the time," he says, eyes streaming. "But usually out the front. Pretty sure it's the neighbour's, two doors down."

"How about you, James? Is he pulling my leg?"

"I've seen it too," he says. "Surprised you haven't."

"Well, in fairness, my window faces the back. But yeah, thank fuck for that. Don't think my heart could take any more shit right now."

Seventeen

Sometime in the small hours of Wednesday morning, Naoka's eyes snap open and she slips naked from beneath her bed covers and puts her feet on the floor. The house is deathly quiet, the others no doubt sound asleep, as she opens her door and creeps out onto the landing.

Going up the narrow, twisting staircase to Stanley's room, she pauses outside his door and places an ear against it. The scent of the anointing oil still lingers, sweet and a little unpleasant, and she wrinkles her nose before turning the handle and stepping inside.

A thin light steals in from the terrace, the room a tapestry of charcoals, blacks, and blues, and as she approaches the bed, Stanley stirs and mumbles before turning to face the sloping wall.

Slowly lifting the covers, she gets in beside him and runs a hand down his side as far as the waistband of his briefs. She tents her fingers and slips her hand inside, creeping around the curve of his hip until she finds his penis in its nest of pubic hair.

Stanley wakes now, feeling her warmth against him and quickly becoming erect as she strokes the underside of his shaft. Her breath on his ear and neck has an unpleasant, almost rotten smell, but in his growing ardour he pushes the thought aside and twists his head to kiss her.

Naoka pulls away from him and moves beneath the covers, easing his underwear off. Then she kneels between his legs and takes him into her mouth, her teeth grazing the head and the upper part of the shaft.

Moaning low, almost sighing, he revels in the warmth of her lips and tongue as her head bobs up and down with increasing purpose. So much for staying in her own room at night, he thinks with a satisfied smile.

Feeling him swell almost to bursting point, Naoka moves up his body and guides herself onto him, inching slowly down until their pelvises meet. She places her hands on his chest now, resisting his attempts to pull her towards him and kiss her, then begins to gyrate her hips.

Thrilled by her silent, wide-eyed intensity, Stanley allows her to dictate proceedings, focusing only on the pleasure of her hot, tight vagina. But as his sap begins to rise and the fear of coming too soon invades his thoughts, that awful feeling of dissipation rears its ugly head again.

Naoka feels him start to slacken and grunts in displeasure.

Sensing her frustration, Stanley tries desperately to regain the moment, but he loses it completely when she reaches down and grabs either side of his head. Her touch feels cold now, almost cruel, as she grinds her pelvis hard against him.

"Fuck me properly, little boy," she hisses.

"I'm trying, Nao."

And gripped by a sudden, blinding rage, she twists his head with a surge of inhuman strength. The damp crunch of his breaking neck brings an instant hardening of his cock, and he spurts inside her as she rides him to an obliterating climax of her own.

Slowing now, she gazes down at his stricken form and feels her mouth become a grin. His cock is still stiff, a rigid stick of dead meat, as she lifts herself off him and fumbles around for his briefs. Using them to wipe herself, she tenses the muscles of her abdomen, the remainder of his semen spilling onto the soft, stretchy cotton. Then she pushes them into his mouth, a darker hole in the inky blackness of the room, and clambers out of the bed.

Closing the door behind her, she creeps downstairs, her face awash with silent tears, and a minute later she's back beneath her own covers and drifting down into dreamless slumber.

Eighteen

At the end of her second lecture, Sadie makes her way to the student bar to meet up with the others. Tomorrow being a day off for all and sundry, they plan to make the most of it with a couple of cheeky drinks.

"No Stanley?" she asks, finding them at one of the larger tables in the corner.

"Haven't seen him," says Luke.

"Neither have I," adds Naoka, gazing absently at the flip phone in her hand. "Not since last night, anyway."

"I'll bet, nudge nudge, wink wink."

"To be fair, though," says Sharon. "He didn't seem all that interested yesterday."

"Maybe he'll join us later."

"Hopefully so," says James. "He's actually quite a laugh with a beer inside him."

Sadie makes her way to the bar, accompanied by Sharon, and they stand and chat while the barman deals with a handful of other orders.

"So," she says. "Anything happening with you and James?"

"Oh, don't."

"Come on, spill the beans."

"Nothing to spill," Sharon says with a knowing smile. "At least not yet."

"Just try not to fuck it up like you did with that Dave guy."

"Course not," she says. "What a sorry saga that was."

"What's with Nao, by the way?"

"What do you mean?"

"Just seems a little off. Maybe she's had a row with Stanley."

Over at the table, James and Luke discuss the night's festivities while Naoka stares into the middle distance. They'll nip into Bestmart for more beverages, then order a takeaway and maybe watch a movie. Not another horror, though, that's for sure.

"Plus, I managed to score us a bit of weed."

"You're a legend, my boy. This is going to be a blinder."

"Got you all another," says Sadie, placing a tray of drinks on the table. "Beers for the boys and a Juicer for her royal Naoship."

"Cheers, dears."

"Thanks, Sades."

"What do you fancy for tonight?" asks James, sipping his beer. "Chinese or Indian?"

"Naoka-san, she no wike Chinese."

"You can piss right off with that bullshit, Luke."

"Woah, okay," he says, taken aback by the sharpness of her tone. "Guess I need to get some better material."

***

The five of them were warming up by the time they left the student bar, and the mood is buoyant as they pile into the living room of number thirteen. And after a few more drinks, James gets the weed out, with only Naoka not eager to partake.

"I'm a lightweight anyway," she says. "I'll only end up with my head in the toilet."

"Come out to the kitchen at least," says Sadie. "No good four of us being out there, and you being in here on your own."

"Still no news from Stan the man?"

"I'm not his keeper, Luke."

"Alright, sorry I spoke."

They drift out to the kitchen and sit at the table, James and Sharon on one side, drinks flowing, eyes glowing, Luke and Naoka on the other, and Sadie at the head.

"I propose," says Luke, "that we smoke in here. Should be okay, as long as we open a window and close the door to the hallway."

"Seconded," says Sadie, adding tobacco and weed to a king-size rolling paper. "I don't mind going outside if it's only me, but since we're all partaking…"

"Any decision on the food?" Sharon asks.

"I'm all for a curry," says James. "But maybe we should wait until after the weed. You know, let the munchies call the shots."

"Fine idea, my boy. Come on, Sades, you're taking forever with that thing."

"Cigarette tobacco's too dry and crispy. Shame Stan the man's not here. His rolling baccy would be ideal."

"Has anyone checked his room?" James asks. "Maybe he's up there and doesn't know we're back."

Naoka's stomach lurches at the suggestion, although it really would clear things up. The longer the day's gone on, the less sure she's become that last night's dream was actually a dream. But she just can't bring herself to go and look. What if he's lying in his bed there, stiff and dead?

"Hallelujah," says Luke as a spliff of sorts is finally produced. "Even though it looks like a sleeping bag."

"Fuck off, will you? I'd like to see you try."

"Better than I could manage."

"Thank you, James," says Sadie, lighting the spliff and taking several tokes before passing it on. "Now if someone would be so kind as to open another bottle of wine."

Luke stands and goes to the fridge. "Oh. My. God."

"What?"

"Only sixteen beers left."

"You dick."

"Have some of this, mate," says James, holding up the spliff and spluttering a little. "Not as good as the last stuff, but better than nothing."

And so the weed is smoked and the drinks are drunk, and an hour goes by in the blink of an eye, except for Naoka, in whose case it feels more like ten. She really must go up and check. It's stupid sitting here with a face like the back of a bus when all she needs to do is confirm the obvious. Stanley's out, or he's busy with his books and not in the mood for socialising with a group of legless teens.

"You okay there, Nao?"

"Just a bit tired, Sharon. Might head off to bed in a while."

"We haven't even ordered food yet," says Luke. "Come on, grab another drink and we'll go back to the living room. Don't know about anyone else, but I'm freezing my ass off in here."

"Seconded."

"That's your second seconding of the night, Sades."

"Well, don't expect a third."

"You lot go ahead," says James. "I'm going to have a go at rolling one of my own. Can I borrow your lighter, Sades?"

"After losing my last one?" She hands him the rolling papers and a couple of cigarettes. "There's matches in the drawer, mate."

"I'd better stay and lend some moral support," says Sharon. "Let us know if you're going to order food."

Nineteen

"I'm a bit worried about Nao," says Sharon, pouring another glass of wine. "She's not her usual self at all."

"Maybe she and Stanley had an argument."

"Yeah, that's what Sades said."

It's on the tip of James's tongue to mention his misgivings about Stanley's absence, but he doesn't want to kill the mood. The way things are going right now, he and Sharon might actually get it on, so he opens another beer and pushes the thought aside.

"I was thinking," says Sharon, "and I know it sounds stupid…"

"Go on."

"But when the priest woman was here, what was her name?"

"Reverend Black or something."

"Yeah, well, it felt really good. Like when I was a kid and we used to say the Lord's Prayer and sing hymns in assembly. That feeling that there's a higher power watching over you."

"Well, I don't—"

"I know what you're going to say, James, but just for now, just for tonight, can you keep it to yourself?"

"Okay."

"I mean, that feeling you have when you're a kid, nothing fancy or complicated, just this simple understanding that of course there's a God. I really miss that."

"Actually, that's beautiful," he says, his eyes on her lips. "Do you want to share a bit more of that spliff? I've hardly got anything off it yet."

"Yeah, sure."

He takes it from the ashtray, wasting a handful of matches trying to get it lit, then hands it to her.

"It's better than Sadie's," she says, taking a second, deeper toke. "But if you say that in front of her, I'm denying it."

And with more weed and booze under their belts, it's only a matter of time before the inevitable happens. Sharon gazes at him, and when he leans in, their mouths finally come together, and in the heat of the moment she doesn't notice his vile breath. She murmurs in pleasure as he strokes her neck with one hand and cups her midriff with the other.

"Know what would be wonderful?" he whispers in her ear.

"What?"

"Taking one of those kitchen knives and cutting out

your chitterlings."

She pulls away frowning, and he grabs the back of her head and slams her face onto the tabletop, knocking her unconscious. Then he stands and goes to the knife block on the counter, which used to house eight but now houses only five. Selecting the longest and sharpest, a ten-inch chef's knife, he holds it up to the light, his grinning mouth contrasting with the horror in his wide, unblinking eyes.

"Just the thing," he says, "for butchering a nice ripe sow."

***

"Taking their time out there," says Luke. "Maybe I should go and check on them."

"And end up cock-blocking poor old James?"

"What do you mean?"

"Fucking hell, Luke, you really are dense at times."

"Ohh," he says, after thinking it over for a moment. "Really, James and Sharon? He never said anything to me."

"As if he would," says Naoka, a slur in her voice as she nears the end of her drink.

"Hey, that's not—"

"No, no, I don't mean there's something wrong with you, Luke. I just mean guys aren't so good at talking about matters of the heart. He probably didn't even mention it to himself."

"Do you think he'll be a knob to her?" Sadie asks Luke.

"If they start getting serious, I mean."

"Nah, I don't think so. He's always been—hey, did you hear that noise?"

"Probably James banging his head on the table because he still can't get a spliff together."

"Maybe I should go and check."

"Fucking hell, Luke, no. They'll be back in soon enough, unless they take it straight upstairs, I suppose. Kitchen's like the Arctic with that window open."

***

Still unconscious in her chair, head resting on the kitchen table, Sharon doesn't see James approaching with the knife. If she were to struggle now, his careful yet powerful stab might miss its intended target. As it is, the point goes clean between the two vertebrae in her upper back, severing the spinal cord and killing all sensation from the neck down.

"Better when they feel the pain," he mutters. "But if the others hear, it might just spoil the fun."

Gagging her with a tea towel, he wrestles her onto the table, flat on her back, then comes around the side. He pinches the first of her eyelids and lovingly slices it off, repeating the process so that both of her eyes are fully exposed. And now she's beginning to stir, turning her head from side to side, her face a bloody mess.

When Sharon finally regains her senses, her head aches

to high heaven and there's something terribly wrong with her vision. Her eyes are stinging and sore, and only if she really screws up her face can she dim the invading brightness of the light above her.

"Hmm mmph."

"Oh, good," says James, unbuttoning her blouse. "I was worried you were going to sleep through the whole affair."

"Hmm mmph."

"..."

Sharon raises her head and manages to partly clear her vision by vigorously rolling and swivelling her eyes. And what she sees makes her scream into the gag, forcing bubbles of mucus out of her nose. James, towering over her, eyes wide open, knife in hand. And as he brings it towards her body, she tries to struggle and is horrified to find she can't move a muscle. From her neck down there seems to be nothing but radio static.

Humming a low tune, James drives the point of the knife into her solar plexus and slices downwards with a steady motion, like opening a particularly juicy pie. Blood wells up dark and rich, Sharon's muffled screaming and the thrashing of her head doing little to disturb his merry endeavours. Yet, another part of him longs to look away as a second, crossways cut is made and the glistening, throbbing innards start to bulge out.

In a frenzy of fear, Sharon starts banging the back of her head against the table, filling the room with noise. Her heart pounds and her ears sing with a wild rushing of blood, until James puts the knife down and aims a blow at the side of her head, once again knocking her unconscious.

And now it's time to get his hands properly wet. To have a good old rummage around in her living flesh and find a tasty morsel or two. A little treat before he can finally drive his blade up beneath her ribcage and watch the light seep out of her eyes.

***

"Hear that? More banging."

"Sounds kind of, you know, rhythmic," says Sadie. "Maybe they're..."

"I'll never eat at that table again."

"You'd think they'd have the decency to do it upstairs," says Naoka, getting wearily to her feet. "Talking of which, I reckon that's me for the night."

"Not sticking around for food?" We can order it now if you want."

"I'm not really hungry, Luke, but thanks anyway. And I'm sorry for snapping earlier, even if it was a shit joke."

"That's alright. I kind of was a dick."

"See you in the morning, Nao," says Sadie. "Sleep tight."

And with that, Naoka steps out into the hallway, glancing at the unfamiliar sight of the closed kitchen door before heading up to her room. But as she goes to enter, the thought of Stanley intrudes on her heart and mind for the thousandth time today. She really must check.

So, climbing the stairs now, a disturbing parallel to last

night's awful dream, she switches on the landing light outside his room and draws several trembling breaths. Dear God, what is she going to find in there? A greying corpse with a pair of her underpants stuffed in its mouth? Oh no, don't let it be that. Don't let her have done that to him.

Finally, when she can bear it no longer, when the need to know outweighs the fear of finding out, she steels herself and opens the door. And no, it can't be, can it? The bed is empty. Dear God, it was just a dream all along. A rush of sweet relief, of pure unbridled elation, comes washing over her, and she doesn't see the figure lurking in the shadows.

***

It takes a while for James to come fully back to himself, to truly feel his blood-soaked hands and forearms, to register the bitter-sweet taste of Sharon's liver in his mouth. And with the return of his faculties, the sheer horror of the scene before him hits him like a ton of bricks.

Sharon lies there on the table, her intestines and organs bared, like some disgusting parody of that kids' operation game. And as he looks at her in stomach-churning dismay, her ruined eyes slick with blood and tears, he sees that she's still alive, her chest rising and falling faintly.

What has he done? What has he done to this beautiful girl who he's spent the last five months wanting to kiss? Why, he's carved her wide open and spilled her innards everywhere, that's what. And by the looks of it, eaten a hearty portion of her innards.

And now, in a moment of crushing clarity, he knows what he has to do. There's no way on earth that either of them can come back from this. Even if by some miracle she survives, she'll be a physical and mental wreck, and as for him, he simply can't live with what he's done.

So before she comes around again, before she has to face another second of fear and pain and confusion, he takes the knife and slides it up into her heart. And sobbing now, silently, achingly, he twists the blade and sees the life bleed out of her.

And now it's done, there's only one more step to take. Crossing to the sink, he wets his hands, gone sticky with drying blood, and from somewhere upstairs comes a long and piercing shriek. But that's no longer any concern of his, and he goes to the toaster, turns the socket on, and rams his dripping hands down into the slots.

Twenty

As Naoka backs away from Stanley, or the thing that used to be him, she shrieks again. She never had herself down as a horror movie cliche, but there you go. Besides, it's not every day you see a reanimated corpse with a broken neck and a raging hard-on.

To keep Stanley's head from lolling around, the thing is holding it up by a fistful of hair. A pair of crusty briefs dangle from its mouth, and the image might be comical if it weren't for the eyes, which gaze at her with icy, gleeful malice.

Continuing to back away, she loses her footing and ends up flat on her arse, banging her head against the terrace door. The thing takes another step closer, not at all dissuaded by her vain attempts to kick at its legs, and that's when the house goes dark.

In the faint yellow streetlamp glow coming in from the terrace, the thing looks even ghastlier still. Its eyes glint cruelly and its face has a sickly, waxen look. And as it reaches down, the briefs fall out of its mouth.

Gagging from the smell of its breath, an almost visible current of stench, Naoka tries to stand, only to find that her legs have given up the ghost. The thing seizes her by the lower jaw, its dreadful touch making her shit herself there and then, and lifts her to her feet with outrageous strength.

Unable to open the terrace door, both of its hands being occupied, it begins to slam her against it. The first two attempts put cracks in the glass and almost knock her insensible, and the third drives her right the way through it and up against the terrace railing.

***

When the lights went out, Luke was already heading upstairs towards the source of the shrieking, and Sadie was on her way to the kitchen to fetch the others. But now she retraces her steps to the living room and retrieves the torch.

Flicking it on, impressed with its bold white beam, she heads back down the hallway and pauses outside the kitchen door. It's a bit quiet in there, isn't it? You'd have thought they'd be venturing out or at least making some kind of noise.

So it's with great trepidation that she opens the door and trains her torch beam around the room. The first thing she sees is a gleaming pair of eyes, causing her to flinch and almost drop the torch, and when she looks again, hands trembling, taking in not only the face but the butchered body, she doubles over and vomits.

When the waves of nausea have finally passed, she straightens up again, eyes streaming, lips a sour and slimy mess. The wavering torch beam moves to the right now, never to look upon the horrors of the table again, and eventually picks out James. He lies on his back just beyond the fridge, one leg bent beneath him at an impossible angle, and he seems to be holding something in his lap. And when Sadie looks closer, she sees it's the toaster, more or less welded to his hands, deep and livid burns going up both of his forearms.

"What the hell happened here?" she mutters, but her mind is streets ahead of her mouth, and she can piece it together well enough. "Dear God, James, what the fuck did it make you do?"

Then the distant sound of breaking glass snaps her into action, and she decides that, like it or not, the electricity has to go back on. Whatever Luke's dealing with upstairs, he won't be helped by the darkness, that's for sure. So with a heart that couldn't sink any lower without falling out of her asshole, she goes and opens the cellar door.

***

After turning an ankle on the last flight of stairs, Luke limps cautiously into Stanley's room. And despite it being pretty dark in here, the source of all of the shrieking and the breaking glass is as plain as plain can be.

"Fucking hell," he shouts, going to the shattered terrace door and pulling it open. "Let her go, Stan, for fuck's sake."

Naoka is bent backwards over the terrace railing, eyes bulging out of her darkening face as Stanley squeezes her throat. For whatever reason, his other hand is on top of his own head, and it's such a strange sight that Luke actually catches himself in the midst of a double take.

Then, as though wishing to welcome the new arrival, Stanley swivels his head completely around with a twist of the arm and wrist. Stunned by the sight, not to mention the cold, almost laughing eyes, Luke stumbles back.

And with a mad surge of energy, Stanley redoubles his efforts to throttle Naoka, and the terrace railing gives way. For a moment they seem to hang in the air, the railing swinging out to the side, then gravity steps in and the two of them tumble out of sight.

Going to the edge of the terrace and peering down, Luke is met with a most appalling spectacle. Stanley and Naoka are impaled through their chests, one atop the other, on the iron spikes of the garden fence. In the glow of the streetlamps, he can see blood spilling out of her gaping mouth. Such a fetching couple, he thinks, a smile beginning to form on his lips.

Twenty One

The cellar may have lost some of its smell, being that Charlie's bowels were apparently part of the issue, but Sadie's stomach still wants to disgorge itself again. And as she surveys the electrical panel, the turncoat bastard that it is, she takes great pains not to let the torch beam wander down there.

Looks like only one trip has gone, apart from the main breaker, and she figures it must be for the kitchen, given what she saw of James and the toaster. So she resets it then pushes the main breaker up, expecting the lights to come on, but nothing happens. And when she removes her hand, it springs back down to the off position.

"Jesus wept," she says. "I guess he totally fried the wiring."

She tries the breaker a few more times to no avail, then goes back up to the cellar doorway and calls for Luke. The house is silent now, as still as the grave, or at least most fucking graves, but as she strains her ears, she hears footsteps coming down.

And it is now that the feeling strikes her again, the one she felt at the station several weeks ago, the voice saying run run run and never look back. But time is short, and the footsteps have almost reached the ground floor now, and fuck fuck fuck, Sades, it's the cellar or nothing, girl.

So she kills the torch for a moment and steps backwards, closing the door behind her and creeping down to the ghastly darkness below, each creak of the stairs threatening to betray her whereabouts.

***

Well, a game of hide and seek might actually be quite jolly. The girl can cower and snivel down there while he slowly turns the screw up here and regains some energy. Inhabiting that corpse was a foolish mistake, far more exacting than these weak-willed adolescents.

So he hobbles to the front door and turns the deadbolt, snapping the key off in the lock, then goes to the living room to commence the seeking. Where are you, little piggy? Where are you, dearest? And he takes a peek through the window at the bodies skewered on the fence. Looks like the ching chong is getting a decent swiving at last.

Next he roots around the office before opening the cellar door, pretending a change of mind and going into the kitchen. Oh, there she is, the sweet young sow, her exposed eyes almost luminescent in the gloom. And reaching down now, he gouges one out and pops it into his mouth, thrilling at the meaty crunch and the still-warm jelly within.

Gouging out the second eye, he turns his attention to James. It seems the boy chose to put an end to himself. Not quite according to plan, but hardly the end of the world. And anyway, the girl down there should more than make up for it. So he locks the back door, once again snapping off the key, and pauses for a moment to survey the carnage on the table there while tucking into the second eyeball. Now then, now then, what happened to that knife?

***

While the thing possessing Luke clumps around above her, Sadie takes a reluctant, torch-lit tour of the cellar. It seems there's really not much down here, just a series of rough brick walls and pillars, plus a couple of bits of furniture even more shabby and knackered than what's upstairs.

There's also a load of brushes and rollers and tins of paint in the space beneath the staircase. And among them she finds something that might, just might, get her out of this unholy mess. Well, either that or burn her to a crisp. But it has to be worth a go, and what's the alternative? Wait around like a lamb about to be slaughtered?

It sounds as though the thing is up in the office now,

making way more noise than Luke ever would. Surprisingly light on his feet, that one, considering the size of him. And now there are footsteps in the hallway, and the cellar door creaks open, almost forcing her heart clean out of her chest. But then the door closes again, and the thing goes into the kitchen, where poor old James and Sharon lie all mangled and mutilated.

And now Sadie can feel herself beginning to slide into that vacant state, just like when she found her mother, and she knows deep down it will be the death of her. Plenty of time to process this shit if she manages to make it out of here, but right now her life depends on keeping it together. This bottle of paint thinners isn't going to open itself now, is it?

Twenty Two

When the cellar door comes open a second time, Sadie knows the shit is about to hit the fan. All she can hope for is that this thing doesn't notice the fumes coming off the thinners, which are as strong as hell and starting to make her lightheaded.

"Little piggy?" it says with Luke's vocal chords. "Our game has almost run its course, I fear."

Sadie stands stock still, afraid of the crampy legs that squatting down would bring. She only has one chance here, and fucked if she's going to ruin it by getting sloppy right at the death.

"But worry not, we'll stretch it out as best we can." The thing is coming down the stairs now, scraping what sounds like the tip of a knife along the brickwork. "And what I did to the others, well, that will pale in comparison to what I'll do to you. Cut off your teats and shove them up you, little piggy. By the end, you'll be begging me for death's sweet embrace."

"Sounds great," she says, voice quavering despite her growing sense of resolve. "And what are you going to do after that?"

"Now that would be telling."

"Can you hear me, Luke? Are you in there somewhere, mate?"

The thing stops several stairs from the bottom and stands in silence, apparently mulling the question over.

"If you are, don't you think you should fight this bastard?"

"He can't, little piggy," it says in mock regret, creaking down the last few stairs. "But it isn't farewell just yet. He'll be joining us for the show."

And as the thing stalks towards her, Sadie shines the torch beam into its face. It pauses just where she wants it to, and she can see as clear as day that Luke is well and truly gone, the eyes cold and hateful, the mouth a cruel, vicious leer.

"Why are you even doing this? Some sort of deal with the Devil?"

"Oh, the Devil can choke on my root." It starts to chuckle now, low and guttural. "The pain and suffering have always been their own reward."

Wishing there was something she could say that would even get close to her contempt for this thing, this sadistic piece of shit that murders and maims for the sheer hell of it, she drops to one knee, her cigarette lighter in hand.

"For what it's worth," she says, striking it against the

linoleum floor, "you sound like a massive twat with all that piggy stuff."

The puddle of thinners welcomes the flame, and she takes the rest of the large plastic bottle and splashes it over what used to be her friend. Blue then yellow and orange, the flames rise thick and fast, and with only their light to guide her, she darts past the burning figure and makes a lunge for the staircase.

In her mind's eye, the thing should be screaming by now, but instead there's almost silence, just the crackling of flames in the glow behind her as she throws herself up the stairs. And she's almost at the top when its burning hand closes around her ankle and the knife blade plunges into the meat of her thigh.

"Get the fuck off me," she shouts, twisting now and lashing out with her free foot, kicking its face until the flaming flesh begins to slough away, revealing the skull beneath.

Breaking its grip at last, she scrambles up the last few stairs and into the hallway, and as it follows her out on its hands and knees, she slams the cellar door into its head and shoulders.

Limping hurriedly to the front door now, she's horrified to find that she can't get it open. She turns back to see the thing shambling towards her, slashing wildly with the knife, and aims a desperate, furious kick at one of its knees.

As it crumples back, its leg giving way, she rushes into the living room and begins to lift the heavy window sash. The thing lurches in from the hallway in hot pursuit, its eyeballs boiling and bursting, and hurls itself blindly at her, slashing her shoulder to the bone.

She snakes around and shoves with all her might, and it falls back onto the corduroy sofa, sizzling gobbets of fat coming off its ruined body. And finally, finally, finally, the room filling with smoke and flames behind her, she gets the window open just wide enough to slither out into the night.

Twenty Three

The sight of Stanley and Naoka, a hideous kind of fusion yakitori, should horrify Sadie to the core, but she's too hopped up on adrenaline for anything to touch her. Sharon splayed open like that, James quite literally toasted, not to mention Charlie's twisted face and Claire's throat hanging open, like some wild animal had been at it. And now the stink of paint thinners and burning flesh and rendered body fat, and the deepening pain of her wounds as the cold night air begins to probe them.

So yeah, the point of dismay has been well and truly surpassed, and all she wants now is a quiet minute and a cigarette. She limps her way down the path as the sound of sirens springs up in the distance, no doubt some neighbour calling the police after getting an eyeful of the two young lovers on the fence. The next thing will be the fire brigade, no doubt, what with the flames in the house going up so rapidly.

For the authorities, the truth of what happened here will always remain something of a mystery. Sadie will cooperate as best she can, but they will be left with the feeling that some key information has been withheld. And in years to come, the first officer on the scene will tell the tale of 13 Cromwell Lane, of the bruised and bloodied young woman he found at the garden gate, cigarette in hand, watching the blaze with wide-eyed wonder.

Acknowledgements

Heartfelt thanks to the following fine people, without whom the lot of an independent author would be a whole lot lesser: Ellen Joyce, for unflinching and insightful advice on the early drafts—you very much rock; Dennis Klatt for support, suggestions, and friendship throughout the entire process, concept to completion—I owe you a drink or ten; Bolivia Fang and Dannah A. for taking the time to read and comment on the penultimate draft—you're both superstars; and of course, my wife and children, who always give me the time and space to write—I adore you all.

About the Author

Born and raised in Plymouth, England, Jan is a father, a husband, and a former poet. Readers enjoy his work for its directness and sense of humour, as well as its smooth, free-flowing prose. This is his first novella.

Printed in Dunstable, United Kingdom

64674439R10071